Deli Ideology: A Novel

Deli Ideology: A Novel

GRACE JUNG

Thought Catalog books

Brooklyn, NY

Contents

Part III. PART THREE

Part 1

PART ONE

"I haven't any allegiance, any responsibilities, any hatreds, any worries, any prejudices, any passion. I'm neither for nor against. I'm neutral."

–Henry Miller, *Tropic of Cancer*

1

The Interview

"Where do you see yourself career wise?"

The interview begins as soon as I take a seat inside Linda's office. It is brightly lit with fluorescent tube bulbs that hover over her. The skyline is visible through the window. The view stretches all the way downtown, and a part of the Hudson is visible on the right. The prospect of a sight like this five days a week excites me a little bit.

"I don't know. Something involving office hours, I think."

"You want to teach?" she asks me, head bending down a little bit her eyes still on me.

"Not really. But it beats working five days a week."

"What did you study in college?"

"Comparative literature."

"And you said you went to Korea for a year?"

"Yes."

"And is that where you're from?"

Her hair is big, brown and curly. She's wearing lots of mascara and plum colored lipstick. She's wearing a woman's suit. The color combination is as follows: red, blue, yellow and green. She's wearing big gold earrings. They are orbs encircled with twisted silver.

"Yes."

"Are you a citizen? Will there be any visa problems?"

"Um, no. My father was naturalized when I was in high school."

Linda is white but her last name is 'Lau.' When I received the email for an interview with her, I assumed she was a Chinese-American attorney, but no, she is Jewish.

"Were you in Korea to study languages?"

"To translate fiction."

"When did you get back?"

"About a month ago."

"Is literature what you want to teach?"

"I don't know."

"Okay. Well, LJ, you seem like an intelligent girl. And, look, even if you don't want law to become your career, it can still be a good experience for you. It's a pretty universal field. Now, you said you worked at a law office for two years?"

"When I was an undergrad, yes. Part-time."

"And what kinds of things did you do there?"

"Drew up contracts, affidavits, transcribed letters, proofread, that sort of thing"

"Okay, so LexisNexis and all that, you're familiar with it?"

"LexisNexis, yes."

"And now you work as a PR assistant?"

"Yes."

"Why do you want to leave that position?"

"Because they pay me by the hour and I don't make enough money to keep up with my expenses."

"How much do they pay you there?"

"Eleven an hour."

"And you make enough?"

The room feels small. Linda's desk seems too cluttered. I don't feel as nervous as I did when I first entered her office.

"No, actually. I put in weekend hours at a deli by Herald Square."

"What do you think you can bring to our litigation firm?"

"A college degree, and competency in writing and analytical reading."

"I see. And why are you looking to work here?"

"Money."

"Well, money's important."

"Yeah."

"Okay. So let me tell you a little bit about what we'd expect from you. You'd be working with our other paralegal who has been with us for two and a half years now. I think you spoke with her—Georgina?"

"Yes."

"She's been the sole paralegal here the entire time but she really can't handle everything on her own. You'll be helping us by booking our flights and hotels. I don't need to be pestered with questions on what sort of conveniences I'll need. Twin bed, single—whatever's fine. I really don't care where I'll be staying, as long as the hotel has a bed and there's a car waiting for me outside in the morning. There are thirteen partners here at the firm. Most of us have at least two kids. As you can see, I am six months pregnant, and this is my third child."

I do see. She is very pregnant. I can't imagine what it must be like to carry weight like that all over the city. I can't believe she's done this twice before.

"If we need to be reminded of something, it'll be your job to do so. We don't need to be asked about anything so long as things run smoothly. It's your job to make sure we don't have to deal with trivial matters. We have enough to worry about."

"Of course," I say without blinking.

"You can go to Georgina if you have any questions. Anyway, like I said, you seem smart enough and pretty reliable."

"Thanks."

"How much are you looking for in terms of a starting salary?"

"Mm…"

"Just an estimate."

"Well, I would trust that your firm's offer would be an appropriate sum to justify the amount of responsibilities handed to me. I'm not worried about it."

"We can offer you twenty-eight thousand as a starting salary. You get seven days of paid vacation. We don't offer health insurance until your second year with us."

"I see."

"Alright, so, why don't we have you come in to meet the partners next Monday or Tuesday? It'll depend on what I hear from your references. I'm sure I have nothing to worry about."

"Okay."

"Thanks for coming in. Talk to you soon."

I leave the office and pass a couple of rooms full of white middle-aged men and women. There are fourteen partners at this firm, I hear, and Georgina is the sole paralegal. I would be their second.

Back at the front desk is Georgina—the chick who emailed me—a white girl with big brown eyes and a purple summer dress.

"How did the interview go?"

"Good."

"Great. We'll speak to you soon then."

I take the elevator down to the lobby. The ride is quick. While my ears buzz with an ominous hum, it feels like my bladder is getting pushed up into my stomach. Then my ears pop. Outside of One Penn Plaza, it stinks again. A man is sleeping with a blanket over his head next to a rosebush by the building. Tourists amble about in one giant pack with their big families stopping only to photograph one another in front of Madison Square Garden.

2

The Extra Hours

Working seven days makes one forget what to make of leisure. Time stretches like taffy. All the events get jumbled. Things that happened just yesterday feel like they've happened a month ago. It's hard for me to keep track of events while locked in a constant routine of work and without a day of rest.

From Monday through Friday I do some copyediting at a PR firm in the Upper East Side. Each day, I wake up at seven then I'm out the door by eight thirty. When I arrive at the office, I sit at any empty desk I find for eight hours, proofreading human resources letters written by pharmaceutical companies that explain why the company will be cutting back this quarter. I can feel my body repelling the labor. My joints ache. My mind is tired. I want to do nothing by the time I get home. All I want to do is eat something with a lot of flavor and watch something loud on my laptop screen in my room at the apartment I share with my roommate Annie—a big white girl who wears raggedy pink cotton slippers around the apartment and a white bathrobe with ice cream cones all over it. She has small green eyes that slant upwards, the kind of eyes that kids used to make at me with their fingers on the corners of their eyes, except these were actually Annie's eyes. It's as though she'd pulled them back to insult an Asian person at one point and then they stayed that way.

No. Annie's cool. She's so relaxed from all the pot she smokes. Her tiny brunette girlfriend Maggie is cool, too. She comes over and talks on the phone a lot while chain-smoking Marlboro reds.

Annie is a year older than I am. She graduated Dartmouth and majored in sculpting. At the moment, she's a temp at an office in Brooklyn where she applies her skill in graphic design towards advertisements for vegetable seeds and locally grown produce. I think she kind of feels the same amount of confusion and uncertainty as I do at times, but she doesn't seem bothered or nervous by it. Probably because of the constant smoking she does.

Annie keeps her pot well maintained in beautiful small jars with tin lids that screw on tightly so that the contents remain sticky and fresh. Every once in a while she takes a jar out of her dresser and shakes it while grinning at me. This indicates that she wants me to smoke with her.

3

Twenty-three

My friend Chuck called the other day—a screenwriter in his mid-thirties based in California. He said that his younger brother called him earlier that afternoon, yelling about his frustrations at the DMV. Chuck complained that his kid brother was a childish idiot who didn't know anything about the world. I had to remind Chuck of something very important: his kid brother indeed *was* a childish idiot who didn't know anything about the world because he was twenty-four years old. The inconveniences of our system are not so very obvious to those who are used to them. People forget.

"How old are you now, LJ?" Chuck asked me.

"Twenty-three."

"You're so young. At your age, you should be sleeping with a lot of different men and taking lots of drugs. That's what I did when I was twenty-three…" Chuck said.

"Right," I said.

"After you sleep with him though, don't linger. If he offers you a cup of coffee, take it, then say, 'bye,' and go. Just leave."

I had nothing else to say. I wondered what sorts of drugs he was suggesting that I take.

"After my stepfather passed away this year, I went back to Georgia to check on my mother. She was crying, telling me what things he'd left behind, etcetera, and then she mentioned pills. So of course I went into his medicine cabinet and took what was left."

"What kind of pills were they?"

"They were just sedatives. They make you very drowsy. Anyway, I'll be in town soon. I'm flying out tonight. I'm staying with a filmmaker in Brooklyn. I'll call you when I get there."

"See ya, Chuck."

4

Making Moves

My mind feels overcrowded lately. It's like my head is a desk full of pages and pages of paper with a bunch of chairs crammed underneath it as if too many people were supposed to sit there all at once. I feel like I can't really think or make decisions for myself. As much as I want to figure out my next move and just go there, it turns out that moving is not so easy.

Nothing is going as planned. Twelve publishers turned down my translation manuscript, which I completed at the end of my yearlong residency in Seoul. They said that the content was fine but that no one cared to read what Korean writers from the colonial occupation had to say. I don't disagree completely, but it's hard to just let a pile of labor simply go to waste, unread and unappreciated. At what point should I give up on the prospect of a career as a translator and writer? At what point do I say that enough is enough and settle for twenty-eight grand a year with no benefits just to work as a paralegal at a litigation firm with fourteen partners? At what point does one give up?

5

Saturday, August 21, 2010

It's five a.m. when the alarm goes off. I shower and get dressed in a pair of jeans and a red T-shirt with the word 'KOREA' on it. By the time I step out of the building, the sky isn't as dark anymore. Just a moment ago, from my sixth floor apartment window, the sky was dark blue. It's lighter now, but I can still see the moon. I look past the black contours of the trees and the leaves in the playground across the street. The sky there is darker than the east side of the street. I make my way westbound then south. On my left, past the cars driving down FDR highway, the light creeps across the East River and makes its way towards my direction. I continue to walk south watching the sky change colors with every block. It grows lighter and lighter. By the time I reach Herald Square, the Empire State building is covered in orange light. I cross Broadway, past the tables and chairs and pigeons, and several men and women sleeping outside on benches. Some of them move and stretch. I see one man doing sit ups on the sidewalk.

When I walk into the deli, it's six fifty-five. Mr. Bae is counting bills at the register. I give him a quick bow and greet him in Korean. He nods his head at me. I walk to the register counter opposite from the main register and tuck my bag into the shelf space under it next to the cardboard bin full of plastic utensils. I take two hair ties from my wrist and tie my hair into pigtails, letting them trail down my chest.

"Good morning, Mr. Bae!"

I turn around and see Meeja waltz in with a black purse over her shoulder. She joins me behind the counter.

"How've you been? Been good?" she asks me in Korean. I bow and say, "Yes," before walking to the other side. Meeja grabs a red T-shirt from underneath the counter and heads into the restroom in the back to get changed. I ask Mr. Bae how his night shift went.

"I'm so tired," he says. "Fought with so many customers."

"What happened?"

"Last night, this girl comes in and hovers over the hot foods. She grabs a piece of chicken from the buffet with her hand and starts eating it! I say to her, 'What's your problem? You have to pay for that!' And you know what she says to me? 'I'm just trying it. I'm just tasting your food to see if I like it or not.' Can you believe that shit?"

"Damn."

"She's just trying... People are crazy," he says. Mr. Bae takes the wad of cash and ties a rubber band around it. He puts it into a brown paper bag and stuffs it into a cardboard box, way below the shelf under the register counter.

"That's for Mr. Choi," he says to me.

"Okay."

Mr. Bae walks over to Meeja and greets her. He tells her the story he's just told me. I look to my left and see Jose making home fries.

"Hola, Jose!" I shout.

Jose turns to me and waves.

"¿Cómo está, mi amor?"

"Bien, bien."

Mr. Bae continues his rant:

"And, I swear to god, last night, every single drunk son of a bitch in the city wanted to use the bathroom. Every single asshole that walked into the store asked for the bathroom key. After the hundredth time, I just hid the key and told them it was broken. Some asshole threatened to piss on the floor."

"Rotten bastards," Meeja says.

Mr. Bae grabs a plastic bag from underneath Meeja's register counter and walks to the back of the deli and into the bathroom. He returns, changed into a white polo shirt. He waves at me and Meeja and tells us to have a nice day.

A Latino man in his late forties walks in with a green backpack and the *New York Post*. He has gray hair and a mustache, with a gold chain around his neck. He waves at me.

"Morning, Sandy," I say. Sandy orders a toasted butter roll at the deli counter. Jose pulls out a sheet of wax paper and slides it over to Arnold, while saying something to Sandy in Spanish. Sandy laughs. Arnold chuckles. Sandy walks to the coffee dispensers across the floor from me and fills a ten-ounce cup full of coffee. He adds half and half, pours sugar into it and brings it to the register. Sandy is fifty-something-years old and works as a security guard at Hotel Pennsylvania. He always has a tired look but never fails to have something to talk about.

"I'm gonna have it to stay," he says. He looks down at his watch. "Yeah, to stay. I have some time."

"One ninety-one," I tell him. He hands me two bills. I punch the numbers into the register and click ALT. I pull out a dime and hand it to Sandy.

Arnold puts the roll on a Styrofoam plate and onto the orange tray. Sandy says something to Arnold and Jose in Spanish. Then he says 'thank you' to me in Korean.

"I study languages, you know?" Sandy says to me, taking his time collecting his tray. "I have a fascination with languages." He stops and holds his fingers up in the air, looking at the back end of the deli. Jose turns his head and looks in the same direction, sees nothing, then turns back to Sandy.

"I know some German, some Italian, some Portuguese, and I know the two that you just heard. Plus English."

"That's nice," I tell him.

"Yeah. Yeah…" Sandy finally walks to the back of the store to the seating area, pulls out a chair and sits down to eat.

6

Korea

"Hey, how you doing?"

I look up and see a tall Latino man counting bills in his wallet.

"I'm alright."

"Yeah? Where you from anyway? Are you new?"

The man is wearing a large orange T-shirt and a silver watch with a chain band. His head is shaven around the sides and the top is a flattened curly nest.

"Uh… yeah. I'm new."

"And you're Korean?"

"Yeah."

"Is that why it says 'Korea' on your shirt?" He points at my red T-shirt.

"I guess."

"Good. I'mma have the cheesesteak and this soda right here."

I tap the lemon wedge on the register, grab a plastic bag from below the counter and air it out. I put the two items in along with a handful of napkins.

"Yeah, I need to go go go," he says. He hands me a twenty. I return his change.

"Have a good one," I tell him.

"You too, young lady." He winks at me before rushing out the door.

A Middle Eastern man brings two sixteen-ounce bottles of Evian to the register. I ring them up, accept his cash and return his change. I look up at Meeja. She grabs a fly swatter and hunts around the deli. I turn my head and look outside again.

"Why are you working so hard, LJ? Why not live at home with your parents?" Meeja asks.

"I hate living with my parents."

"You should live at home with mom and dad. Think of how much they'll worry about you."

"They're fine."

Meeja shakes her head.

"Rotten girl."

"Libby got a pretty decent job, didn't she?" I ask.

"Yeah. Who told you?"

"Your ddal. Gina."

"Yeah. They send her home in a limo if she stays overtime." Meeja walks from the main register's platform to the other side, across from where I stand. She grabs a plain Greek yogurt from the fridge and hands me a dollar from her pocket. I punch "1.00" into the register and insert the bill.

"She's lucky. Where does she work?"

"Pharmaceutical company. Communications department."

Right before leaving for Korea last summer, I remember hearing from a mutual friend that Libby was working at Borders bookstore in Fort Lee.

"She's going to Taiwan in the winter," Meeja says. She wipes a spoon on her shirt and opens the yogurt lid.

"That's nice."

"She's going to meet her boyfriend's family. I have to start learning Chinese." Meeja laughs then recites a string of nonsense that's supposed to imitate Cantonese. "But I don't mind that Libby marries someone who isn't Korean. It's not up to me, you know? If Libby's boyfriend wants to be a part of our family, I have to adjust to certain things just like he does. Right?"

"Yes."

"As long as he's not black, I don't care." Meeja puts a spoonful of yogurt into her mouth.

The wall phone's loudspeaker clicks on.

"Send LJ up to the office," a voice says in Korean.

Meeja presses a button and says, "Yes, sajangnim."

She releases the button and looks at me: "Mr. Choi wants to see you."

7

Orange Tree Delicatessen

Orange Tree Delicatessen is located on the corner of Seventh Avenue and Thirty-third Street. It is across the street from Penn Station and Madison Square Garden, a block away from Herald Square, and just a few steps away from Hotel Pennsylvania, which makes it a convenient place for tourists to go to for breakfast, lunch and dinner. It is open twenty-four hours a day, seven days a week. It attracts a number of MTA and Amtrak employees, local construction workers, Madison Square Garden staff, PATH train commuters, employees from One Penn Plaza and thousands of tourists.

The store has been on this spot for fifteen years. It was originally owned by a Polish Jew who owns two other businesses right next door—the Greek and Chinese fast food restaurants. He sold the store to two Korean businessmen who ran the deli together up until five years ago. When the partnership fell through, it was sold to Mr. Choi. Mr. Choi kept the same employees from before, most of whom who had been working here since the day it opened.

The interior has yellow painted walls with various stains and splatters of mysterious gray, red, black and brown matter. The crown molding that borders the walls are painted dark green. The floors are covered in Caribbean-green linoleum tiling. All the colors inside the deli suggest a tropical vacation, but no one thinks that when they enter.

The entrance is made of two swinging glass doors that remain open all year long. There is no lock. Upon entry, to the left is a gelato fridge that carries an assortment of flavors such as coconut, blueberry, strawberry, vanilla, cookies-and-cream, chocolate and coffee. There's a frozen yogurt machine right next to that. A Korean girl, a couple years younger than I am, stands behind it from ten a.m. through seven p.m. on Saturday, Sunday and Tuesday. She has a name but I never remember it so she's just "Gelato Girl" to me.

Next to the gelato fridge and frozen yogurt machine is the register counter and an ice cream fridge with a sliding glass door directly below it. The ice cream fridge is full of King Cones that were once half melted then refrozen back into their separate parts of milk, syrup and ice. Beside them are fruit bars of strawberry and coconut flavors, ice cream sandwiches and plastic cups of ice.

On the register counter is a medley of packaged goods: individual pieces of Ferrero Rocher chocolates that are not supposed to be sold individually, shots of energy drinks, packets of supplementary tablets, cookies, and a basket of detached bananas. The cash register is some old model made in the early 90s. The plastic covering is stained yellow. The fine grooves of the plastic are filled with dirt and grime from numerous hands that have touched it for two decades. The counter itself is dark green. Right beside the register is a scale that weighs food items from the salad bar and steam trays of hot foods at six ninety-nine per pound. Beside the scale are two stacks of plastic orange trays. Directly behind the register area, attached to the wall, is an enormous wooden shelf holding dozens of various brands of cigarettes, chewing tobacco, rolling papers and cigars.

Moving past the register counter is the deli container filled with displays of prepared paninis and sandwiches. Below them are cheeses and deli meats. Attached to the deli case is a bain marie for soups and a wooden prep table where the sandwiches, bagels, and other ready-to-order foods get prepared. The stainless steel prep table has a rotating toaster, microwave, bread cabinet and a deli meat slicer. Beside it is a double-compartment sink with a paper towel dispenser directly above it which is covered with a thick coat of sticky grease. Next to the sink is the deep fryer and grill. The register and prep food areas stand on a slightly elevated platform, which makes the deli employees look about a foot taller than they actually are to all the customers.

Directly across from this section is another register counter with a small open fridge area full of yogurts, fruits and cans of Red Bull. To the right of the fridge is a large counter space with hot water and coffee dispensers, and a large plastic container with three separate spouts for skim milk, whole milk, and heavy cream. Next to that is a hot chocolate and instant cappuccino machine. To the left of the register counter is the wooden candy shelf. Going further left from the shelf is a tremendous fridge with clear Venetian-style blinds that hang down from the ceiling to retain the cool air. The fridge carries dozens of drink selections including beer and wine.

Between the fridge and the wall on the opposite end are two glass cases full of prepared food. On the left side is the salad case with stainless steel bins of chopped lettuce or maraichere greens, pasta salad, tuna salad, egg salad, bean salad, dressing containers, and precut squares of cantaloupe, watermelon, pineapple, honey dew, and individual grapes. All in all, the place is a depressing little space. It's dirty, full of bugs, rodents and bacteria.

Shortly after my return from Korea, I immediately found a place to live on the sixth floor of an old building, located on First Avenue and Seventy-second Street. I used my savings to put in the deposit, and found a job fairly quickly as a copyeditor, making eleven dollars an hour, which was still not enough to make rent. I contacted Gina, a childhood friend who had been asking around if anyone needed a weekend job. I went to trail her at the deli one Saturday afternoon. Gina's mother, Meeja, was also there, and she showed me how to work the cash register.

"Have you used one of these things before?"

"Yeah. When I was a waitress in high school."

"Good. This button makes the register drawer pop. This one is the 'no sale' button. Try to avoid hitting this. If you make a mistake or somebody leaves without paying for the items, push this button and pull out the receipt. Write 'void' on it and put it in the register with the pile of credit card receipts. Try to avoid writing 'void' on receipts. The boss doesn't like it. Whenever you ring up the items, remember to hit the TAX button. If it's a sale with no tax, hit ALT. Now follow me." Meeja pulled out a handful of long, white memo sheets. The backs said "Marlboro" and "Newports." They were originally cigarette cartons. Someone had cut them up to reuse them as memo pads.

"Write down the item prices on this," she said. She handed

me the sheets and a ballpoint pen, and walked me over to the candy shelf right below the register countertop.

"Gum is a dollar fifty. The Tridents are a dollar seventy-five. The Toblerone isn't that expensive. One fifty. The Ritter chocolate is four dollars. The Lindt chocolate is three seventy-five. Now, with drinks." Meeja walked over to the fridge located in the far back on the right-side wall. Beside it was a stairway leading up to the second floor, which was a dining space. On the left side were about a dozen tables and chairs, also a dining space. Two rows of buffet-style prepared foods took over the center space.

"Snapple and all the bottled sodas are a dollar seventy-five. The canned sodas are a dollar twenty-five. These sodas in the aluminum bottles are two dollars." Meeja went through the entire inventory with me.

After I finished writing the prices for everything down, I wondered why anyone would want to spend their money at a deli. The deli charges two fifty for Luna bars, which are sold for ninety-nine cents at healthy and upscale supermarkets like Whole Foods. Even Rolaids cost a dollar twenty-five.

"You want to keep a good relationship with the Spanish kids," Meeja said to me in Korean. "Don't get on their bad side. Treat them with respect and it'll do you a world of good while you work here. Believe me."

"That's not a problem," I told her.

"You speak Spanish?"

"Yeah. A little."

The meeting with Mr. Choi was brief. I requested ten dollars an hour for my services.

"With no cashier experience?" he asked.

I said nothing.

"Starting pay for my people here is eight an hour. But since you are educated, I will give you nine an hour."

"Fine."

I was scheduled to work from seven to seven every Saturday and Sunday, which brought in eight hundred and sixty-four dollars a month to cover my rent and utilities. The rest that I made from the PR firm was put to paying off student loans, transportation and food.

8

A Letter

I step down from the register booth and walk past the deli glass, the salad bar and steam trays. I walk by the seating area which has about a dozen green table tops and red cushioned chairs. A bunch of mirrors hang in the far back wall that makes the deli appear more spacious than it actually is. I jog up a flight of stairs. The second floor has more tables and seats. About sixteen table tops—four of them booths with green and blue synthetic covers over the bench cushions. The tabletops upstairs are dark green, an incredibly mundane color, which is safe because it is just dark enough not to show any stains or dirt. The fluorescent bulbs are dim, and several of them flicker.

I see the tall, old white man with his curly white beard, glasses and suspenders. I don't know what his name is but he always asks for a plastic bag to carry his things upstairs. He comes here every weekend.

"I can't carry the tray," he would say, "because I have a bad knee." The old man is sitting at a booth doing crossword puzzles.

I walk past the restrooms and knock on a gray door.

"Come in."

The air inside is clouded with smoke. The walls are lined with shelves. There's a small dusty fan, an unused computer monitor, a bunch of brown bags with rubber bands tied around them, piles of paper, and about fifty boxes of cigarettes on the shelves. One box is opened with four cartons of Marlboro Ultra Lights spilling out onto Mr. Choi's desk.

"Hi, Mr. Choi," I say.

"LJ, I have a favor to ask you," he says in Korean with a cigarette sticking out of his mouth.

Mr. Choi is very dark-skinned. I don't know where he gets all that sun while sitting in this poorly lit, tiny office all day. He has a bunch of scars on his cheeks and the back of his neck from years of bad acne.

"Okay."

"I need you to write me a formal letter. Now, what happened was, for the last four years, payroll has been giving Arnold about forty-one cents short of what he was supposed to be receiving for his overtime," he says.

"Okay."

"I need you to write a letter saying that we corrected this mistake by fully compensating him at once."

"Okay. But I need to charge you."

Mr. Choi grins, "Fine. I'll pay you fifty bucks."

"Okay."

I sit at the computer and open Microsoft Word. I type out a header with the deli's address, Arnold's full name and Mr. Choi's full name.

Mr. Choi lights another Marlboro Ultra Light. The white smoke twists and coils upward before hitting the ceiling and splitting out in all directions. I type words into the computer like "acknowledge" and "hereby" and "understand" and "compensated." I line up the signature lines with the date and capitalize the names right below them.

"Okay. All done."

"Wow. It takes geezers like us a whole week to write something like this," Mr. Choi says.

"You should give me a raise."

Mr. Choi laughs.

"You said you work at a PR office during the week, right? Monday through Friday?"

"Yes. Nine to five," I say.

"Aren't you tired?"

"I'm fine."

I walk back downstairs and see Jose making French toast and pancakes on the grill. Arnold is lining up the pita bread out on the counter to make panini sandwiches. Meeja is chatting with a customer. I return to the register.

A black man with a knitted wool hat, a beard, and open-toe sneakers brings a carton of Tropicana orange juice to the counter.

"Y'all are making your sandwiches too early. How much for this?" he asks.

"Dollar seventy-five."

"For this, daughter?" he asks me, looking up.

"Yeah. Sorry..."

"It's okay. I'll pay for it." The man takes out a folded dollar bill and unfolds it for me. He hands me three quarters then raises the juice carton, looking at me. I smile and nod. He walks out the door, joins the moving crowd rushing to and fro on Seventh Avenue.

9

A Hill of Beans

There's a great line from a film, starring Nicholas Cage before his acting career began to depress me. It's from *The Weatherman,* and Cage's character insists that he is not a hill of beans and that he has a plan. Of course, throughout the movie, not a single plan he makes works out accordingly. Life, he soon realizes, is as unpredictable as the wind. There's a good lesson to be learned from that film and it is, don't plan because the rest of the world doesn't care that you have any.

A couple of my friends came to visit me in New York the other week. One is from Chicago and the other from Denver, but they met in Korea as English teachers at the same after-school program for elementary school students. They returned to the US and moved in together into some apartment in Chicago three months ago.

I met them at a Japanese restaurant in Midtown. Over sushi and hot sake we discussed the direction our lives were taking, and the economy. Stephanie already seemed to know that I was working seven days but not much more beyond that. Joe pressed me for answers, asking me what I did on the weekends.

"I don't wanna say," I said.

"Why? Are you a prostitute?" he asked.

"No. I just don't wanna say."

"Well, you have to tell us," he said.

I hesitated, and thought about lying.

"I'm a cashier at a deli," I finally told them.

There was a pause.

"Well," Joe finally said, "you'll make it as manager real soon, LJ!" Stephanie laughed. I chuckled along, but I knew that none of us at the table were really any different from the other. Joe is currently unemployed and living off of his savings, which he made back in Seoul as an English teacher. He majored in history in college but he can't write for shit. I've read some of his emails. He misspells homonyms and misuses punctuations, but he loves that semicolon and uses it in every other sentence. He made a ton of money in Korea teaching afterschool English programs because his white skin and American passport were enough reasons to qualify him as a teacher to his employers in Seoul. Stephanie currently fills in as a substitute at an elementary school in downtown Chicago. She needs to wait for a call incase there is a sick leave or absence, but until then, her schedule is just as unpredictable.

Fact of the matter is that being in our early twenties and living in an economically depressed state, the three of us are doing just fine. Our situation is the current American norm. None of us are particularly doing any better or worse.

"You seem alright for someone who works over sixty hours a week, LJ," Stephanie said.

"Thank you."

"There's no such thing as a sure thing at our age," said Stephanie. "You'll figure out what's best for you in your future."

"Thank you."

"Oh, by the way, LJ," Joe said, "Steph and I had dinner with Daniel the night before we flew to Chicago. He says hi."

"Yeah, what's going on between you two?" Stephanie asked.

"Nothing," I said.

"I think he has a girlfriend," Joe said. "He brought her with him the last time we saw him. She's really quiet, but seems alright."

I poured hot sake into my beer and drank.

10

Abandoned Building

LJ touched her chin. There was a zit. It hurt.

The 1221 green bus stopped in front of a bakery.

"This stop is Korean National University of the Arts." LJ swiped her wallet against the bus pass, listened for the beep then pushed out through the doors. As the bus roared off behind her, LJ lifted her leg to check the heels of her shoes. There was gum on the left sole and the heel on the right shoe was worn down. The metal head of a nail was starting to show.

"Fuck," she said.

She heard a bike bell ring. She looked up and saw Daniel biking towards her, standing on the pedals. His brown hair was flat against his head from the wind. His back was arched and shoulders pointed forward. He grinned as he rode towards her in his dark gray jeans, a bright red T-shirt and brown leather dress shoes.

"Who dressed you this morning?" LJ said.

"I did," he said.

"Why did you bike here?"

"This is my new bike," Daniel said, turning the bike around slowly, making a U-turn.

"Yeah, I can see that. Why'd you bike it out here? It's a five minute walk."

"I felt like biking. I'm excited about my new bike," he said.

"That basket looks dumb..." LJ said.

"I know. I have to remove it so that I can lessen the weight."

LJ walked alongside Daniel as he biked slowly, standing on each pedal, letting one leg push down, forcing the chains to turn, thrusting the bike forward, then catching the lift of the other pedal with his other foot, repeating the same motion over.

"Let's cut through here. You know there are hikers here?" Daniel said.

They walked through a small patch of wooded area with manicured shrubs and benches. There was no road except for a sandy path.

"Yes. I know. I've been here before," LJ said, looking at the large mountain that loomed over the campus. Past the yellow security gate, Daniel pointed at this building and that, explaining which one was going to get torn down after being up for nearly a hundred years, and which one was abandoned, and which one was for the dance students.

LJ pointed at it and said, "You like that building."

"I like that building," Daniel said.

"Because it houses dancing women."

"Because it houses dancing women," he repeated.

Daniel led the way into a building and stopped by the convenience store kiosk near the entrance.

He grabbed two ice cream bars and paid at the register, where a young man was watching a show on a tiny television screen.

"Did you know that statistically ice cream sales are higher in the winter than in the summer?"

LJ looked at Daniel for a long time without saying anything. Daniel stared back, then started to laugh.

"Hey! Don't do that…" LJ said, slapping his arm.

"I had you going there for a minute."

"That's from my story. You read my story?"

"I read some of your story."

Daniel continued to walk his bike down through the hallway as LJ followed. The building was silent. The floors were made of cold, brown tiles and the walls were covered with water stains. Daniel lifted the bike and carried it up a flight of stairs. On the second floor, LJ saw a row of lockers painted brown. Daniel opened one of the lockers and kicked his shoes into it. He grabbed a large pair of black Adidas slip-ons and dropped them on the floor. He slipped his feet into them then looked at LJ.

"This way."

He pushed a large swinging door with a small glass window and entered the studio. The studio had a funny smell. Several students were sleeping with their heads on the desks. Others wore headphones and sat at their desks with laptops open.

"This here's my space," he said. LJ took a seat next to his chair. He parked his bike next to it. The cubicle had drawings of buildings, print outs of alternative Korean farming technique designs in mountains, and a large poster with four big lines running across the page, dividing the poster into five segments. The segments were each a collection of small squares and circles drawn inside the squares, like little mandalas.

"That's the Kim Whanki painting on the postcard I gave you," LJ said.

"Yeah. I regenerated it. I made it using Illustrator on my computer. I drew each square and circle by hand but digitally."

Daniel opened a drawer and handed her the postcard she'd given him.

"I like this," LJ said comparing the postcard with the recreation.

"Hold on."

Daniel got up and walked over to a girl wearing a red sweatshirt, sitting at a cubicle on the far right side of the room. He asked her for a screwdriver in Korean.

"What?!" the girl asked.

"A screwdriver," Daniel repeated in Korean.

"Why?!" she yelled.

"Can I please get a screwdriver?"

"You think everything here is for free? You Americans think everything's for free. Nothing in life is free…" the girl said disdainfully, opening her drawer and fishing through it.

The girl handed him a screwdriver.

"Thanks," Daniel said, laughing.

"Go away," she said. Daniel returned to his desk and began to unscrew the basket from the bike then removed it. Then he removed the bottle holder and the bell. Daniel took a step back and studied the bike.

"This is a great bike. It only cost me seventy bucks."

"That's a steal," LJ said.

"I know. I love this bike."

The two walked off campus and entered a Family Mart. They grabbed two bottles of Cass beers and sat outside the mart in plastic chairs and drank. LJ saw a young girl with a red hairband that had tiny red horns that lit up under a battery-charged bulb. She was riding a tricycle, following her mother who walked leisurely up ahead.

"I used to do that back when my family lived in Daegu. My bike had a backseat and my kid cousin rode in it. My dad pulled us from a rope, running. It made us both scream."

"That sounds like a happy childhood," Daniel said.

"No. I was very unhappy as a child."

"Why's that?"

"I don't know," she said. "I was just constantly unsure of everything. Maybe I wasn't unhappy. Maybe I'm unhappy looking back at my childhood. Yeah, that might be more correct."

They sipped their beers in silence.

"I'm having difficulty figuring out what I'm supposed to do," LJ said.

Daniel stared off into the air without saying anything.

"Trying to devote myself to a life of writing and translating other people's writing is depressing. It's hard. I think about all the forms of writing that seem to be dying right now. Like with poetry. I saw this one guy read a poem out loud to an audience while taking all of his clothes off and putting them back on again," said LJ.

"Where'd you see that?"

"At some reading in New York."

"Well, artists are like that. They're constantly innovating. I don't see anything wrong with that."

"It's wrong because it's ultimately dumb. That's why it's dying," said LJ.

"You seem worried about something that doesn't need any worrying right now. What are you actually scared of? An artist's task shouldn't involve being concerned with the stuff you just said. You need to have just one goal and that is to expand your territory out there and in here," he said. At that last part, Daniel moved his hand towards his chest and swept it across.

"Inward-outward process," she said.

"Yeah. The digging occurs both ways."

Daniel sipped his beer and pondered for a moment.

"When I was working on the recreation of the painting, I overheard a professor screaming at his student from the other room during her presentation of a café design. While he was yelling, he said something that struck me. He said, 'An idea is a dot. Identity is the line.' I was really impressed by that remark."

LJ and Daniel polished off their drinks and looked at the sky for a moment. The light was starting to change.

"Hey, do you want to see something amazing?" Daniel asked.

"Yeah."

"Okay, let's go."

Daniel led LJ back onto the campus and into a white building with big round tinted windows, like a ship. He pulled open a brick red door and led her down a dark hallway. LJ saw a few desks and chairs scattered randomly across the floor.

"Is this building abandoned?"

"Yep."

At the end of the hall was an open door. Sunlight streamed in from the outside. There was a bright green lawn, a small crab apple tree and shrubs planted all around the perimeter. A giant white rabbit ran out from a bush towards Daniel and touched his feet. LJ walked up next to him. The rabbit stood up on its hind legs and touched LJ's shins with its paws.

"Oh my god," she said.

"This is Clara the rabbit."

"What's wrong with it?"

"What do you mean?"

"It's too friendly. It's not natural."

"People walk through this atrium all the time just to say hi to Clara and hang out."

Daniel gave Clara's head a gentle pat then walked LJ back into the building. He took her hand and led her up the stairs. The railings were massive. Each bar was a thick twisted steel painted black. The tile floors on the second floor were black and white like a chessboard. The ceiling had loose wires and no lights. The walls of the hallway looked eerie and green in the dark. Daniel pushed a dark door into an empty classroom with three massive, picture windows. The late afternoon light turned the room orange. When Daniel put his mouth on LJ's neck, she gasped and stared out the window at the contours of the trees' crowns lit up by the orange glow. The blackboard against her back felt cold. She thought about the chalk getting on her pants and the back of her head. Daniel moved her towards the wooden desk beside the board to support their weight. Birds flew by. LJ wondered what kinds of birds they were.

In between breaths, LJ asked a question: "What kinds of windows are these?"

"I don't know."

Each time LJ made a noise, it echoed throughout the room.

"Why is this building abandoned?" LJ asked loudly.

"I don't know."

LJ yelled as Daniel came.

The room was dark. After getting dressed, they wandered back out the pitch black building cautiously, embracing the walls as they slowly went down the steps.

"Wait here a minute."

Daniel ran back into the building of his studio. He returned with the recreation of the Kim Whanki painting.

"Here," he said. "You can have this."

"Thanks. What should I do with it?" she asked.

"I don't know. Figure it out."

He led LJ to the main gate and kissed the top of her head before turning back around and returning to his studio.

11

1910

A tall white man walks up to the register in a blue nylon jersey, khaki shorts, and flip-flops. He has big gray eyes that stare straight into mine. He doesn't blink.

"Yes?"

"Camel light," he says in a thick French accent. "And fire."

I turn around towards the cigarette shelf, grab a box of Camel lights and a blue lighter. I slide them towards him.

"Camel lights," I say. "And fire."

"Ah, very well," he says. I laugh.

The man hands me a twenty. I return him six dollars and wait for him to protest that I'd given him incorrect change. So many people from out of town react with outrage at New York City's cigarette prices. But he grabs the carton and lighter, and stuffs them into his back pocket.

"Very good morning," he says. He turns around and leaves.

"Cuantos ahoras, Jose?" I ask.

Jose looks at the clock on the opposite wall with his elbows crossed, leaning against the grill.

"Ten o'clock," he says. I give him a thumbs-up. Nine more hours to go. Arnold is slicing Boar's Head ham with the meat cutter.

A black man in a white shirt, shorts and flip-flops stands before the register, waiting for his order.

"Yeah, ring me up. I'm getting three ham and cheese sandwiches and these sodas right here," he says.

"Nineteen ten," I say. I pull out a plastic bag and throw in a few napkins.

"My grandma was born that year," he says.

"Wow."

"Yeah. She's turning a hundred years old this December."

"Nineteen ten was an important year," I say.

"She's turning a hundred but she still goes around spankin' us like she don't even know we're thirty somethin' years old. She'll come walkin' right up behind you and go whack! Right against the behind. I'm like 'Grandma! Whatchu doing? That's no way to treat a grown man.' But she'll act like she don't even hear me."

"She's a hundred."

"That's right. A hundred-years-old. President Obama sends letters to seniors who reach a hundred."

"Really?"

"Yup."

Arnold hands me three sandwiches wrapped in wax paper. I put them into the bag and hand the bag to the man.

"Have a good one," I say.

"Take care now."

12

Walnuts

"Excuse me," says a sweet old voice with an English accent. I look up and see a tall old white man next to a short, pudgy white woman with red hair and fierce eyebrows that are penciled in dark brown. She smiles at me.

"Yes?"

"How much for your walnuts?" she asks.

"Where do you see walnuts?"

"These here," the man says, pointing to the wines on display next to the yogurts.

"They're fifteen bucks a pop."

"Fifteen dollars, yes?" the English woman asks. I nod.

"Great. I guess we know where we'll be coming tonight then," the man says.

"Yep."

"Cheers."

13

Tuna

"Arnold."

Arnold turns to me and raises his eyebrows.

"Tell me how you make tuna salad," I say.

"It's easy. You just get some tuna, mayo, onions, celery, salt and pepper. That's it."

"No, I want to know how *you* make tuna salad."

"Ah...." Arnold grins. "So, somebody told you, ah?"

Last week one of the cooks downstairs, Naniel, told me that Arnold uses the mop squeeze to drain the excess water from canned tuna. I can envision this very clearly. Fifty-three-year-old Puerto Rican Arnold with his skinny ass legs, high socks and sneakers, his round pot belly hidden behind a red T-shirt, his bald head covered with a white paper hat, and his face, crinkled with thin lines when he grins, as his arm pulls the lever of the yellow mop squeeze covered in gray dirt and god knows what else. When I heard this, I gagged. Then I shouted at Naniel that Arnold needed to be stopped. Naniel laughed and said that I should be the one to say something and stop him: "Because Arnold listens to nobody."

I thought of all the health code violations that this deli was already up to its neck with.

"Tell me, Arnold," I repeat.

"Look. What you do is, you take a *clean, plastic* apron. Not a *dirty* one. A *clean* one. You open the tuna can. You plop the tuna onto the apron. You wrap it up. Stick it in the mop squeeze and pull the lever, and get all that water out."

"Clean, plastic apron does the trick, huh?"

"*Clean.* Apron's gotta be clean," Arnold says. "And when you make a salad, the tuna's gotta be dry. That's how ya get the best tuna salad."

14

Dollar Twenty-five

Meeja walks around the store, stretching out her legs and swinging her arms in the air to keep the blood moving. A white man with fierce wide eyes and a gray beard walks in. He has dark curly hair with some gray showing. He is wearing a tan shirt, a gold chain and jeans. He brings a coffee to the register.

"One twenty-five," I say, punching the numbers into the register.

"What?" the man asks, his eyes opening widely.

"One dollar and twenty-five cents, sir," I say.

Meeja comes to the register.

"Dolla twenty five. One dolla and a quo-ta," she tells the man.

"No. Dollar twenty-five? For *this*?" he says, pointing to the ten-ounce cup. The coffee had spilt some when he carried it from the dispenser to the register.

"Yeah," says Meeja.

"No. Forget it." He drops the coffee on the register and turns to leave.

"Stupid," Meeja mumbles. She takes the cup from the counter and carries it towards the trash. The man turns around and looks at Meeja,

"What?"

"I said stupid," Meeja says.

"No! You don't call me stupid!" The man points his finger at her face.

"You don't know price? You stupid!" Meeja shouts.

The man walks to the register, grabs an orange tray and raises it in the air above Meeja's head.

"Go ahead! You wanna hit me? Hit me," Meeja tells him. She pushes her head towards the man. The man throws the tray down on the floor and points his finger at her face again with his eyes blaring angrily. They look like they might fall out of his head. If they fall, they would fall onto the orange tray.

"You don't call me stupid. You don't call a customer stupid," he says.

"Get out of here," Meeja tells him.

"No. I'm not going anywhere."

"Fine. Stay right there. Stand there all day." Meeja turns her back to him and folds her arms across her chest, looking around the deli.

"I leave when I want to leave," the man says to the back of her head.

"Stay right there," Meeja repeats.

The man turns and walks out grumbling. Meeja picks up the orange tray and places it back on the pile. Pedro brings a stack of orange trays that he'd just finished wiping down and places them on the register counter.

"Thanks, Pedro," I say.

"De nada."

An old white woman with dyed red hair and a gold wristwatch brings a small container of cantaloupes to the register.

"Five eighty-four," I say. Meeja sits back down on the sugar drum and looks out at the store silently.

15

Meeja

I've known Meeja since I was five. My family and I had just moved to Brooklyn, right around the time of the L.A. riots. Watching the news in our one-bedroom apartment, I remember hearing my mother say, "I cannot believe this is happening in America." My dad was eating Sunkist oranges slices and drinking Budweiser from a can. Our living room had one couch, a bed where I slept, and a small plastic toy box containing a remote controlled racecar and Legos that the previous tenant had left behind. Over two thousand Korean-owned stores in L.A. were destroyed that year.

On my first day of Kindergarten at P.S. 127, we stopped at a deli a couple blocks away from my school to get a sandwich to take with me for lunch. The deli was run by Meeja and her husband. They lived inside a two-bedroom apartment which was an annex to the deli. The deli functioned twenty-four hours a day, seven days a week so Meeja and her husband took turns taking shifts, alternating between work and naps.

My mother was twenty-nine years old at the time. She was happy to meet a woman of her own age who had children also. Meeja's older daughter Libby and I became good friends. Whenever my mother went to the deli to chat with Meeja, I went to their apartment and watched videos with Libby.

Meeja's husband was also the same age as my father. Our

families got together for a number of events: Thanksgiving, Christmas and New Year's dinners in the winter, and joint-family vacations in the summer.

A few years later when I entered the third grade, Meeja and her husband moved their deli business out to South Orange, New Jersey. We continued to stay in touch and made the trip out there on summer weekends. At that point, my father was driving a van around the city selling picture frame samples to stores and galleries.

My father was glad to know a fellow Korean man of the same age who understood the working-class immigrant's experience. My mother was just as glad to meet a woman who knew what it felt like to be a young mother, raising children in a foreign country. I owed a lot of my English to Libby and her younger sister Gina who were there to converse with me on our play dates.

Two years later, Meeja and the family left South Orange and moved to Flushing, Queens. Meeja's mother and younger sister moved in with the family to their three-bedroom apartment. The space was very small, and it housed a family of seven. Our family went to visit them one evening, very briefly for dinner. Libby regaled me with the most recent tales of her mother: Meeja had caught a guy spraying e-coli bacteria on an assortment of fruit at the deli's salad bar. The *New York Post* picked up the story and, although Meeja chose to remain anonymous, a picture of her pointing at the salad bar was there in the clipping that Libby had saved. Meeja had also encountered a mugger a couple of weeks prior to our visit; she was walking home after closing up shop when some guy tried to snatch her purse, which Meeja did not let go. She wound up suffering an injury to the eye and still losing her purse. Meeja was also held at gunpoint a couple of times behind the register ever since moving to Queens. She'd lost an entire day's worth of income, which had amounted to several thousands of dollars.

16

Puebla, Mexico

"By the way, does your mother know that you work here?" Meeja asks me in Korean.

"Yes."

"Why don't you find a job at a better place? Libby is making good money right now. Where are you living?"

"Upper East Side. Sixth floor walk-up"

"With a roommate?"

"Yeah."

"Did you try looking for a job?"

"I did. But, I'm not really interested in any of these jobs right now. I want to just work like this, save some money, and complete some projects on the side."

"I see. Okay. Go eat," Meeja says, taking over the main register.

I step down from the platform and walk towards the deli glass.

"Jose," I say.

Jose brings his elbows to the top of the glass and leans over. He raises his eyebrows.

"Can I get mozzarella with lettuce, tomatoes, onions, oil and vinegar on wheat bread?"

"Tostado?" he says.

"Por favor."

Jose pulls out a block of mozzarella and brings it to the meat cutter. He pulls two pieces of wheat bread out of the breadbox and throws them into the revolving toaster oven.

"Oye, Jose," I say.

"Sí."

"How is your son?"

"Good. He go to school soon."

"How old is he again?"

"Twelve. And daughter is…" Jose looks past me and stares at the wall clock for a moment. "…daughter is seven."

"You have a daughter, too?"

"Sí."

Jose's children live in Corona, Queens. Jose lives in Brooklyn.

Jose is from Puebla, Mexico. Two hours drive from Mexico City, he once told me.

"What did you do in Puebla, Jose?"

"I pick beans, corn…" Jose walks over to the toaster oven and grabs the toast. He brings them to the counter and layers the mozzarella slices on one piece.

"Tomatoes. Everything. You know green tomato?"

"Yes. Fried green," I say.

"Sí. Green tomato, corn…"

"Is that better, doing that in Puebla, or this?"

"Ahm… I think this," Jose says, pointing at my sandwich.

"Why?"

"More money," Jose says. He walks over to the sauce section, raises a bottle of oil and vinegar and shows it to me. I nod my head.

"More money…" I say to myself.

"But in Puebla, no work on weekend," Jose says.

"Shit, yeah. That's how it should be," I say. Jose starts to giggle.

Jose works six days a week, taking Sunday off.

"No work weekend. And in Puebla, we work nine to five," Jose says.

"Really? Like an office job?"

Jose nods his head, shifting his eyes a little bit. He looks confused. He wraps my sandwich up in wax paper and cuts it in half. He hands it to me on a small Styrofoam plate.

"Gracias."

"De nada, mi amor."

17

Italian Architects

LJ and Daniel stood outside a building waiting to be buzzed in. It was a firm called Conceptua run by an Italian architect couple who were commissioned by the Italian government to work in Seoul. LJ smoked a cigarette while watching Daniel say 'no' repeatedly to an old lady who was trying to sell him plums.

"I'll give them to you at a good price," she said to him in Korean. LJ peered inside the black plastic bag, which was held open in front of Daniel. She saw yellow plums with little red stains on them.

Daniel averted his eyes and said, "No, we're okay."

"Take some. Take some," the old lady insisted.

"No, we're good," Daniel said, shaking his head miserably. LJ started to laugh. The old woman closed the bag and began to walk away, laughing as well.

Daniel pushed the buzzer again. No answer.

"Maybe they're not in?" LJ suggested.

"I feel bad. Maybe we should've bought some," Daniel said. LJ thought about the plums. They were probably warm from the summer's heat, and moist around the skin from the humidity.

"Oh, here they come," he said. They turned and saw a tall

white couple walk over to them, smiling. They were both carrying black plastic bags.

"Daniel!" the man cried. He shook Daniel's hand.

"This is my friend LJ," Daniel said.

"Hello, LJ. Antonio. This is my wife Maria."

"Hello," said Maria. "Sorry we are late. We were grabbing some lunch from the market. Did they not buzz you in?"

Maria and Antonio led the way upstairs into the building. LJ looked at giant orange posters placed all around the windows, blocking out the sun. The studio floor was set up with big orange desks. Another floor up, there was a giant communal table covered with poster paper, models, printouts, glue sticks and scissors. A girl came out of the bathroom holding a tissue box.

"Hi Jin-young," Daniel said.

"Oh! Daniel! Hi!" Jin-young ran over to the desk space and began to tidy up. She moved all the papers aside and brought out paper plates, napkins and wooden chopsticks from a cupboard. A percolator rested on it.

"Oh my god," LJ said, "you guys have a coffeemaker?"

"Yes. And we have real coffee. From Italy," Maria said.

"We'll have some after lunch," Antonio added.

"So where are you guys coming from?" Maria asked. Jin-young placed paper plates in front of LJ and Daniel. LJ stood up and took some chopsticks and napkins from Jin-young to help. Jin-young smiled and said, "Oh no. It's okay. Sit."

"We were in Chung-muro. LJ wanted to buy a camera," Daniel said.

"Great place. I know a guy there who sells me cheap lenses," Antonio said.

"Oh, I'd like to meet him. I always need someone to sell me lenses at a good rate," Daniel said.

"I went there with Maria a couple weeks ago. They have *everything*. We were looking for black and white film from Kodak. And they had them!"

"They're probably expired, most of those. I bought a bunch without looking at the boxes. They were all expired for at least a year," LJ said.

"Yes, but they're good for a while still," Antonio added.

"That's good to know."

"What did you buy, LJ?" Maria asked.

"Wanna see it?" LJ said, digging into her purse. She produced a blue camera with a large flash bulb and plastic covers.

"Oh, what a sweet looking thing. Is that a lomo?" Maria asked.

"Yep. A toy camera," LJ said.

"Don't call it a toy camera. It's not a toy," Daniel said.

"Well... that's what they're called. Even you called it that," LJ said.

"No. It's not a toy. It's a real camera. You're going to use it to take real pictures. Stop calling it a toy. This is a real camera made for taking real photographs."

Maria and Antonio had stopped speaking. They moved around the room quietly, taking posters from one table and moving it onto another table. Jin-young didn't speak either.

"Okay. I'll stop," LJ said.

LJ turned and looked at the studio's bookshelf. She noticed a spine with the name 'Andy Goldsworthy' on it.

"Hey, I know that guy," she said.

"Goldsworthy?" Antonio asked. He walked over to the shelf and pulled out the book. He placed it in front of LJ and Daniel. They flipped through the pages.

"Thanks," LJ said.

"Who's that?" Daniel asked.

"He's a sculptor and photographer. Really beautiful stuff," Maria said. She took the bean curd pancakes, tofu, chive pancakes and assorted seafood tempura and rationed them onto the plates. Daniel picked up his chopsticks and began to eat.

"He only works with what's there in front of him, usually out in a natural setting. So he uses the raw materials right there in nature," LJ said. "I saw this documentary on him and his work. It was stunning."

"Yes, but he's been getting some criticism lately for his work. They're calling him a cheater," Maria said.

"Cheater?" LJ asked.

"Yes. They think he is straying from working purely with nature and resorting to artificial substances to add them," Maria said.

"Well. If he's only going against principles he had before then, I wouldn't necessarily call it cheating. He's just changing. Or evolving," LJ said.

Maria handed LJ a plate of rice.

"Oh. Thank you."

Maria smiled at her.

Antonio stood up and went into the other room. He returned with a book.

"Daniel, the ambassador's daughter made this portfolio. She

wanted you to see it for some reason. She wants to be an architect and asked you to have a look," Antonio said.

Daniel took the book from Antonio with both hands. He looked through the portfolio. LJ watched as he flipped the pages, one by one, very quickly. Daniel closed the book.

"Looks good," he said. "She should keep drawing everything she finds inspiring."

"I like how visual people use illustrations as journal entries," LJ said.

"Some people have a hard time articulating what they want to say with words so they use visual or physical language. But in the end, they are all meant to communicate," Maria said.

Jin-young gathered the empty plates and chopsticks and tossed them into a trash bin. Antonio took the coffeemaker and went to another room. A few minutes later, the studio was filled with the smell of espresso.

Over coffee, LJ showed Daniel a photo of Goldsworthy's project with snow and animal fur.

"Goldsworthy's a bit of a clown," LJ said. "Look at all the pedestrians. They can't understand why there's a giant snowball out in the middle of the street in the summer."

"Yes, and after it melts, there's animal fur on the streets," Antonio said.

"A sheer clown," LJ said.

"It'd mean a lot to us if you both came to our office rooftop party. It's coming up soon. I'll send you the invite," Maria said.

"Sure. We'll be there," Daniel said.

18

Modern Day

My good friend Lynn applied to nursing school in 2006 because the news kept telling everybody that hospitals were suffering from a shortage of nurses. Being nineteen at the time, she didn't really have any idea as to what she wanted to do with her life. Four years later, as an RN, she now works as an office clerk in the basement of a restaurant in New York's K-Town, counting receipts and handing out paychecks to the Mexican employees on Wednesdays. Most recently, I've been reading articles with titles like, "RNs Can't Find Jobs."

Lynn called a few weeks ago. She said that she handed in a resume at every single hospital in the city, plus a few in the North Jersey area, but hasn't heard back from any of them. She calls me sometimes, in a panic, telling me how screwed she is. I tell her that most of us are in the same situation, working odd jobs to get by while sending out resumes everywhere, hoping to land a job that offers a salary. This is what was promised to us. Instead, we sit on loans and pay them off by working jobs that bring in nine to ten bucks an hour, and commuting from our parents' houses. Either that or move out and work seven days a week and barely scrape by like myself.

I look around and unemployment isn't always the case for all of my friends. My friend Margaret has a degree in design and was employed the minute she graduated college. She's the lucky one, but always has been the lucky one. Margaret's father is a well-off logistics manager for a sugar company based in Jakarta, Indonesia. Throughout high school and college, Margaret had the opportunity to travel and intern at various companies throughout the world every single summer, building her resume, networking and gaining skills that offices would later care about. She is now the assistant art director at an ad agency. She's the only friend of ours who is under the age of thirty and living in TriBeCa.

The difference between Margaret and me is that Margaret was born and raised in circumstances that best fit the system we live in today, whereas I was and still am stuck in the cycle that most blue collared families get stuck in: making just enough to get by but never quite enough to get out of debt completely.

19

Muriel

"Do you know whatever happened to Muriel?" Meeja asks me in Korean. I watch her take her foot out of her sandal then slip it back in as she leans against the counter, letting one foot dangle off the platform ledge.

"No."

"She's probably dead by now, right?"

"I don't know. I think so…."

"*Dead*, right?" Meeja repeats, looking at me with a sorry expression.

"Yeah. I guess. I called her apartment once several years ago but somebody else picked up, saying we reached the wrong number."

Meeja clicks her tongue.

Back when my parents were driving around Brooklyn, visiting retail stores with a pre-owned Ford van covered in graffiti to sell pieces of frame mold samples to galleries, Meeja introduced my mother to a woman who lived on unemployment checks from the government. She was a widow in her fifties named Muriel, who lived around the corner of Meeja's deli with a black cat named Tammy.

"Muriel once showed me this enormous lump on her stomach," Meeja says, rubbing her belly. "I told her that she should get it checked out because it wasn't normal. Her doctor told her that she needed surgery."

"Didn't Muriel have, like, a million health problems? She was a diabetic and on the donor list for a kidney transplant," I say.

I remember the time when Muriel took me to a hospital in Sunset Park. She had to go there for blood work. Afterwards, Muriel took me to a small church where she sat and prayed. I sat next to her, folded my hands, closed my eyes, and said some things silently in my head. After we left the church, she treated me to Italian ice. I got cherry flavored. She got lemon. As we walked back to the apartment, we saw a fat white man wearing glasses, a wife beater and boxers sitting on the terrace with a giant red parrot. The parrot kept saying goodbye to us.

"When Muriel was at the hospital, she asked me to go feed her cat," Meeja says. "Her apartment was so messy, I couldn't even think straight. You turn on the light and see a hundred roaches scatter."

Muriel had a numb left arm. She held my hand once and I dug my fingernails into her palm to hear a reaction.

I asked her, "Did you feel that?"

"Honey, I told you that that arm's numb."

"Did you feel *that*?"

"Numb means I cannot feel," she said.

"I just pinched you real hard."

Muriel said that her husband once stabbed her left arm with a pencil. I asked her if she thought that that was what caused her arm to go numb. She said that she didn't know. Her husband suffered from schizophrenia and he died in a mental institution when he was thirty-three. Muriel was twenty-seven at the time, and left to raise a young daughter on her own. After my family left Brooklyn, I never saw Muriel ever again.

20

Trojans

A small Chinese girl walks in and goes straight to the buffet area. She hovers around the chicken and broccoli, fried rice, lo mein, and Buffalo wings then walks back to the register. She waves her hand at me to get my attention.

"Can I help you?"

She says something to me in Mandarin.

"Can I help you?" I repeat.

She points up at something behind me. I turn around and look at the rows of cigarettes on the wall shelf. I look back at her and touch the cigarette boxes.

"Which one?" I ask.

The girl shakes her head. She points upward. I turn and look up at the row of Trojan condoms hanging from nails sticking out from the wooden shelf. I point up at them and look at the her. She nods.

"Which one?" I ask. I touch each color while looking at her. Blue. Red. Gold. Purple. Black. Then back. Black. Purple. Gold. Red. Blue.

The girl makes a very large invisible box with her hands. I grab the black box of Trojans that say "Magnum" on the front and slide it towards her. Then I change my mind. I raise the condoms into the air and shout at Meeja who is working the register on the other side.

"Ahjoomah, how much?" I ask.

Meeja looks up at me then immediately back down.

"Four ninety-nine," she says.

"You heard the lady. Four ninety-nine," I tell her.

The girl begins to wave her two hands at me, palms forward, shaking her head like crazy.

"What the hell do you need, sweetie?" I ask.

She points up at something behind me again. I turn and look up at the section above the condoms. I see green packages of Always pads.

I grab the closest one that I can reach. The girl starts shaking her head again. She makes another large invisible box with her hands, indicating that what she needs is something very large. I return the pads back on the shelf directly above me, reach to my far left, grab a pack of Always overnights and stick them in a plastic bag.

The girl hands me a ten-dollar bill, receives her change then leaves the store with the pads inside a white plastic bag. I return the black box of Trojans back up on the shelf behind me.

"Next."

21

Jose's Girlfriend

Jose hands Meeja a ten-dollar bill. Meeja gives the bill to me.

"Jose is buying lunch for his girlfriend," she tells me.

"Oh, that's so sweet."

"Yeah. She works around the corner at the fabric store."

I watch Jose put two paninis on the press then walk over to the salad bar. He puts pieces of cantaloupe, strawberries, red grapes, honeydew, and pineapple into a large plastic container then brings it over to me.

"How much weigh?" he asks.

"Don't worry about it, Jose. The ten should cover it."

"Okay. Gracias."

Jose and his girlfriend live out in Brooklyn, and his two children live with their mother in Queens. I once asked him why he didn't marry the mother of his children.

"When I go see her, I see her with another baby. It not mine," he told me. "So I too much cry, so I leave. Live in Brooklyn."

Jose brings the sandwiches over to the register. I put the sandwiches in one bag and the fruit inside a separate bag. I reach over to the right side of the counter and pick up two Ferrero Rocher chocolates, put them inside the cold bag, and tie them up.

"Pedro!"

Pedro rushes over to the front of the store. I hand him a pink receipt with the address on it.

"You know where this is?" I ask him.

"Yes."

"Okay. Here you are. Thanks, Pedro."

Pedro leaves the store. It's very bright outside. The front of the store is slowly getting warmer. I click on the fan. Gelato Girl stares at the light, daydreaming.

22

Gelato Girl

Gelato Girl is from Cheonan. She has reddish-brown hair that she dyes, and she annoys me.

Whenever I go to the sink behind the Gelato freezer, she spreads out both of her arms very widely and doesn't let me pass.

"No!" she yells, and has this amused look on her face. But I'm never in the mood to play games with her. I never laugh when she does this, but she does it all the time anyway. And I go to that sink at least four times a day to wash my hands.

Gelato Girl studied English at a university in Korea and is fairly fluent. She comes to me for advice on how to write her English paper every once in awhile. She currently attends Hunter College to earn her qualification to teach TOEFL back in Korea. The English language is a tremendous commodity in South Korea and other parts of the world.

The old Gelato Girl, Yoon-mi, is on the same career path, except that Yoon-mi is ten years older and has a master's degree in sociology. Yoon-mi was promoted to a cashier's position a couple weeks ago, which is good because she couldn't handle scooping out frozen Gelato all day. She'd hurt her wrist pretty badly one afternoon and dropped three hundred dollars just to get her hand wrapped in gauze. She paid out of pocket because she didn't have health insurance in the States, and the deli did not cover any work-related injuries because she is not a citizen.

"Unni," Gelato Girl calls out to me.

"Hm?" I say without looking at her. I stare at the row of yogurt cups on the fridge shelf straight ahead of me. Gelato Girl pokes her head past the frozen yogurt machine and leans over to look at my face.

"If a sentence in English has the word 'either' in it, it shouldn't be followed with 'and,' should it?" she asks me in Korean.

"Um… It would depend on the structure of the sentence, but yeah, generally it's 'either, or.'"

Gelato Girl has very big teeth, and a lisp.

"Okay." I step down from the register platform and walk down the aisle, lain with green tiles. I walk around to stretch my legs. Meeja sits on the sugar drum, spacing out.

23

Rome

"I read something interesting the other day," Daniel said.

The sunlight was streaming in from the giant glass window beside him. Through it LJ could only see sky, and the tops of four-story buildings, telephone poles, street lamps and tremendous knots of a million black wires suspended in between poles. LJ and Daniel were sitting at a second story café in Itaewon overlooking the street. LJ sipped the last few drops of her mocha latte.

"What?"

Daniel reached into his backpack and pulled out his notebook.

"I liked it so much that I wrote it down." Daniel read the passage aloud:

"...suppose that Rome is not a human habitation but a psychical entity with a similarly long and copious past—an entity, that is to say, in which nothing that has once come into existence will have passed away and all the earlier phases of development continue to exist alongside the latest one... if we want to represent historical sequence in spatial terms we can only do it by juxtaposition in space: the same space cannot have two different contents... it shows us how far we are from mastering the characteristics of mental life by representing them in pictorial terms."

"Ok. What's it mean?" LJ asked.

"It means that the city is telling us a physical story. Everything around us is communicating a message about its past. A city like Rome has changed over time and the civilization allowed it to but Seoul isn't allowed to do that. Everything here gets torn down completely and then something new and shallow and meaningless gets put in its place. History is erased completely from the map. Isn't that sad?" Daniel asked.

"I guess so. I don't know," LJ said.

Daniel and LJ said nothing. The music in the café was blaring a fast pop song by 2NE1. It didn't match the mood that Daniel was in, which LJ could sense from across the table. LJ lowered her mug and stirred the syrup at the bottom of her mocha. They were clumped together into waxy pieces. LJ looked up at Daniel who suddenly looked very troubled.

"Reminds me of a line from *Manhattan*. Woody Allen's character complains about everything that's being forgotten or erased in his city. He can't stand the sight of buildings getting torn down. He says that when he lay down to demonstrate against it, a police officer stepped on his hand," LJ said.

Daniel chuckled as he looked down at his cup.

"But I think it's good to analyze and mourn loss. You sound motivated and like you're at work."

"Yeah. I'm just getting frustrated a bit," he said.

A giant blue bus pulled up at the stop directly outside of the café. Three young women in dresses and heels boarded, followed by an old woman carrying large tote bags filled with small black plastic bags.

"Knowing how to cope with and mourn loss is a very

mature thing. I don't think I could handle it. When I broke up with my last boyfriend, I erased everything about him from my life. I threw away any physical object that he ever gave me to remove the trauma from my life. I didn't know how to deal with it," said LJ.

"That's scary. That's a scary thing to do. But I think I understand you."

Daniel looked around the café. The shiny wooden floors reflected the light coming off the bulbs hanging from the ceiling. A young couple with matching tattoos carried a tray with a sandwich and two mugs into the smoking section of the café. The sliding glass door opened at the push of a button. After the couple entered, the sliding glass door closed.

"I think it's trauma that causes erasure. If it's in the mind of someone who knows of it, who carries it around with them then it's never really erased. Just because the physical disappears it doesn't necessarily mean that the idea of it or the memories associated with it disappear. The people carry them and people can be objects of history."

"Yeah but the people die."

"People can write. They can record. They can film it, photograph it," LJ said, "and those records become objects themselves. I mean, I can understand the harsh feeling of something getting taken away suddenly. When something that was there is no longer there anymore, it's painful. But you'll get over it in due time," LJ said.

"You make it sound like I was in love with those buildings," said Daniel.

"No. *You* make it sound that way. I'm just trying to empathize, and cheer you up a bit. You seem so angry lately."

"I'm angry. I am angry at how inconsiderate people can be. How people can discard history and labor, and not feel any remorse."

"Oh."

"The people here don't know how to mourn loss. That angers me. All the shit they design and build are so shallow. They're so meaningless. They can't understand how to address human touch in their work. This frustrates me a lot," said Daniel. He leaned back into his chair and touched his head.

LJ looked at his chest for a minute. It said, "Pepsi" in white letters across his blue cotton T-shirt.

"It's only possible to mourn loss when people believe that it is a loss. Maybe it is but maybe it isn't. How do you know what these people felt in that space? You should read the story I'm translating now. The protagonist is this young teenaged girl who was married off to a much older peasant man, and he rapes her every night. She associates the pain of rape to the room and eventually burns the house down. There's no way for you to be conscious of everyone's experience and memory and how they feel about the space they are in."

"What about the people who've been in a house for a really long time? Like, for generations? What about those people getting pushed out?" Daniel said.

"What about them? Displacement is a very familiar idea. People here are aware of it, and the displaced people throughout the world are certainly aware of it. You'll find that people mourn loss only when the thing they are used to seeing disappears from their sight. We don't necessarily get attached to the things that we see. The pain is from that thing being in our memory when it is not actually in sight before us. Establishing the new doesn't mean it's wrong. It seems wrong but the new will eventually be old and that thing will be mourned once it gets torn down, too. Isn't that your job? To conceive something newer and better?"

Daniel brought the mug to his lips and tipped it back, then realized it was empty and set it down.

24

Ice Cup

A skinny black man in his late twenties walks up to the register, saying that his soda is too warm. I walk out from behind the register, slide open the freezer compartment glass, and hand him a plastic cup full of ice.

"How much is it?" he asks.

"Don't worry about it. Enjoy your soda."

"Thanks, miss." He turns and leaves.

An old white woman with dyed blue hair and a titanium cane dangling from her spotty wrist places a plastic container with a single chicken leg inside of it. The tall skinny man walks back in.

"Hey, miss," he says. "I work at Sketchers around the corner. Stop by anytime and I'll give you an employee discount."

"Okay, thanks."

He gives me a wave and leaves.

"Well, that's nice," the old woman says to me, grinning. I don't say anything in response. I tap the lemon wedge with my two fingers, grab a plastic bag and air it out. I put the small container with a single chicken leg into the bag and hand it to her.

"And napkins," she tells me.

I grab a handful and drop them into the bag.

25

Cantaloupe

"LJ, did you fight with a black woman last week?" Meeja asks me.

"Yes."

"Over what?"

"She wanted to charge two dollars on her credit card. I said no. She gave me a hard time so I gave her a hard time. Then she cursed at me and insulted my mother. So I told her to go fuck herself."

"Mr. Choi was asking me about it. And that woman came looking for you."

"Okay."

"Hey, how often does your mother get checked for breast cancer?" she asks.

"I'm not sure. I don't really ask."

"You should ask. You should." Meeja taps her feet a little against the platform edge.

"My friend working downtown has breast cancer," Meeja says, switching to English.

"I want to help but I cannot help her," she says. "That make me sad."

"I'm sorry to hear that," I say.

"Me too."

A young black man wearing a red hat carries a container of cantaloupe pieces and red grapes to the register.

"Stay or to go?" I ask.

"To stay. And I'm waiting on a ham sandwich," he says.

"Jose!"

"Four ninety-five," Jose replies.

"Thank you!"

"De nada."

"That'll be ten oh-nine, sir."

The man freezes and says, "Ten dollars? For *this*?"

"Yes."

"Uh-uh. No way. I'm takin' out the fruit. Lemme get the sandwich. Jesus. *Ten oh-nine* for lunch? Please."

The man reaches into his back pocket and pulls out his wallet. He hands me a five and I return his change.

Meeja takes the container and moves it over to the other register, mumbling something.

"What's that?" he asks.

"I have to throw away," Meeja says, raising the fruit. "Because I cannot put this back in salad bar."

"Oh, for real? Alright then. I'll buy it. Yeah, let me have those," he says, reaching for the container.

"You're a nice guy," Meeja says.

"Yeah. It's alright. I'll take 'em." The man pays for the container of fruit at the other register. Meeja asks him where he works. He tells her that he's staff at Madison Square Garden.

"Oh-h-h-h. Very nice," Meeja says.

"Yeah. Yeah. Come by sometime. I'll show you around."

"Okay. I come by. You show me everything there."

26

Waste

"When somebody brings too much food and doesn't want to pay, it's your job to get them to pay. If they bring too much and tell you they can't pay for the whole thing, take off a dollar. If they still complain, take off two dollars. Get them to pay. That's your job," Meeja says. I don't say anything.

"I'm serious. That's a part of your job. Otherwise, Mr. Choi loses money. And it's a waste of food."

"I hate it when people do that," I say.

"Me too. If someone takes too many packets of ketchup or mayo, charge them an extra fifteen cents. If they want another plastic bag, charge them five cents. If they want refills for their coffee, charge them seventy-five cents. All this stuff is a part of the expenses," says Meeja, waving a plastic bag in the air.

"Okay."

An old white lady with wisps of white and blond hair, red glasses and a yellow coat brings a blueberry muffin to the register.

"Two dollars," I say.

"Can I get a bag?" the old lady asks.

I bag her single muffin into a white plastic bag and hand it to her. She drops a handful of change into my palm. I count six quarters, two nickels, three dimes, and ten pennies.

"Can you double bag that?" she says. I look at Meeja. Meeja looks at me and says,

"Tell this grandma that she is harming the environment," in Korean and walks away.

"Ma'am, you are harming the environment. There are polar bears drowning and monkeys falling out of trees because of you," I say.

"I'm paying for this. I have the right to ask for a bag," says the old lady. "You're very rude. You shouldn't speak that way to your customers."

"Have a nice day," I say.

"You shouldn't speak that way to your customers," she repeats. The old white lady wobbles out of the store with her muffin inside two plastic bags.

"Next."

"We're back sooner than we thought." The Englishwoman whose husband had called the wines "walnuts" stands in front of the register with a bottle of Pinot Grigio. She slips a finger into her wallet and waits for me to tell her how much.

"Fifteen bucks," I tell her.

"Bucks, is it?"

"Fifteen."

"Would you mind opening that for us, dear? We'll be drinking it right away."

"Sure."

I reach behind me and feel for the corkscrew on the ledge below the cigarette shelf. I uncork the bottle then put it into a brown paper bag.

"Are you wrapping it up for me so I don't walk around looking like a drunk?" the Englishwoman asks.

"That and I don't want you to get a ticket."

"Ah."

The woman fumbles for the proper bills. She eventually hands me a five and a ten.

"Your bills are very different from ours. They're all the same color," she says.

"Yeah. But they're working on it."

I've been noticing that the bill colors have changed a bit. The fifties have red and blue on the face side, the fives are slightly pink, and the tens are a bit orange.

"If you look closely, they do have different faces and colors," I say. I hand her the brown paper bag.

"Thanks, dear." The Englishwoman joins her husband who is standing outside waiting. I watch them walk away with their bottle.

27

Hapcheon

It was humid, June and morning. Daniel met LJ at the Nambu bus terminal at eight AM. He walked to a fast food counter and ordered a cheeseburger, fries and a soda. LJ asked for orange juice. As soon as they got their food, they boarded.

"Koreans hate me for being foreigner," Daniel said as the bus pulled out of the terminal.

"You're a foreigner in Korea, but you're not a foreigner back in the States. Anyway, don't take it so personally. It's not like you don't benefit from being white here."

The bus moved onto the highway. It entered a tunnel and everything grew dark.

"I like these tunnels," Daniel said.

"They tunnel through mountains because there are so many mountains in Korea."

"Why can't we just drive over the mountains?"

"Why drive over it when you can just drive through it?"

"True."

The bus left the tunnel. Small cars in white, silver and black surrounded the bus on the highway. Trees flew by on the side.

Beyond the highway, there were fields. The soils were tilled and ropes were strung down the field, separating them into rows.

"What are those?" Daniel pointed and asked.

"They're herb fields."

"How do you know? What's under those black net things?"

"Ginseng. I'm sure. Those things cost a lot of money at department stores. Someone gave them to me as a gift recently but they're bad for me 'cause I'm always overheated."

Daniel raised his camera and snapped a photo of the black-netted crops that speckled the field.

"I read an article in the *New York Times* about a Korean woman and her Indian friend getting verbally harassed on the bus in Seoul because the woman was with a non-Korean man. The same article indicates that the nation's number of non-Korean residents is over a million while the country's population is less than fifty million and shrinking because couples in Korea are less inclined to have children and are more career-oriented.

This idea of 'the other,' has two polarized views in Korea. One is hatred among those who are anti-foreign and the other is awe among those who admire foreigners for being something different from Korean. Both discrimination and admiration of foreigners are forms of rejection. Ultimately, a foreigner is not Korean, therefore complete acceptance of a foreigner into Korean society is impossible.

The only way to handle this is to move forward and forget the whole idea of acceptance versus rejection completely. Illustration and expression should be a constant event in order to promote diverse views. Never settle on a single thought. Once any sort of definition is established for someone or some race or some country or some ideology, it should be broken down and forgotten. Get rid of it immediately after it's built. Find another thing to build."

"I like that. Build something and then destroy it and then build a different thing elsewhere," Daniel said.

Daniel and LJ saw bright green stalks of young rice growing out of the watery marsh in perfect rows in the distance.

"What are those little blue houses there?" Daniel asked.

"Someone told me that they house ducks. And in the summer time, the ducks are let go in the rice patties to swim around and eat insects to act as natural pesticides."

"That's amazing."

"Yeah. I know."

Daniel and LJ got off at the Hapcheon bus terminal.

They walked across the street and boarded a smaller, local bus that ran from the main town and into the villages spread out in the outskirts of the town.

28

"Gotta Go"

An Indian girl stands in line for ten minutes with a container of eight dollars worth of strawberries and a bag of Cape Cod potato chips.

When it's finally her turn at the register she says with a little dance, "I have to get on the bus."

"Uh-huh. Ten twenty-seven," I say. The girl takes a few steps back with the container still in her hand, leaving the chips on the counter. She looks out the door.

"Gotta go," she says. She chucks the strawberries into the fridge behind her and runs out the door. Meeja comes to the register and asks what the hell that was. I tell her that she was in a rush to catch the tour bus and that she'd stood in line for nearly ten minutes, but just didn't make it.

"Rotten girl," Meeja mumbles. She reaches for the strawberries buried beneath the heap of yogurt cups, flung here and there. Meeja stacks the yogurt cups one by one, rearranging them by flavors—cherry, blueberry, plain, French vanilla, and assorted fruit. She takes the strawberries and heads back towards the salad bar. The Indian girl runs back in.

"Hi, I am back." She turns around and puts her head into the fridge, looking for the strawberries she had tossed. She begins to move the yogurt cups here and there. Some fall over.

She's making a mess again. I point towards Meeja's direction. Meeja walks towards the front of the store with the container of strawberries in her hand. She hands them to the Indian girl.

"You leave this?" Meeja asks the Indian girl.

"Oh, thank you! Yeah. I was in a rush before. I had to run," the girl explains. I ring up the items again.

"Where are my chips?"

"I don't know," I say.

"Okay, just these then."

"Eight eighty-eight."

While she fumbles for her wallet, I bag her strawberries and throw in a napkin and fork. She hands me a ten. I return her change and she leaves. Meeja sits beside me on the sugar drum, leaning her back against the wall.

She shakes her head saying, "Rotten girl." I laugh again. The line gets longer.

"Hey. Hey you," a Filipina calls out to me. She is middle-aged.

"Yeah?"

"What so funny?"

"What do you need?" I ask.

The woman places a Styrofoam container on the scale. The total comes to thirteen twenty-seven.

I ring up the numbers and hit the tax button.

"Fourteen forty-three," I say.

"Hah?! That thing say six ninety-nine!"

"That thing is the scale, ma'am. It always says six ninety-nine because that is the fixed rate per pound," I say.

"Ah…" The woman looks down at her wallet then looks up at me, chuckling.

"I want to get a co," she says.

"A what?"

"A co."

"You want a *Coke*?"

"Ah! Yes. Co."

"Can or bottle?"

"What?"

I make a gesture with my hands and produce an imaginary can.

"Can," I say. Then I widen the gap between my two hands a little to show her the size of a sixteen-ounce.

"Bottle," I say.

"Ah. Bottle. Bottle."

"Okay. Wait here."

I walk to the back of the store towards the fridge. I see Pedro wiping the orange trays, grinning at me.

"Hola," I say.

"Hola, bonita."

I grab a Coke bottle from the fridge and bring it back up front. I ring up an extra dollar seventy-five. She hands me a fifty. I return her change.

"Next!"

A tall black girl wearing blue-framed sunglasses and earphones brings a Zico coconut water to the register.

"Three dollars," I say. The girl ignores me. I wave my hand to get her attention. She pulls out her left earphone.

"Huh?"

"Three dollars," I repeat. She hands me her money. A young Latino man right behind her puts his Styrofoam container on the scale.

"That thing costs three dollars?" he asks the girl.

"Yeah. These people fuckin' robbing us," she tells him.

"Whew." The man shakes his head.

I bag up the girl's coconut water.

"Thank you," I say.

"Mm-hm." The girl sticks her earphone back in and walks out.

"Is this to stay or to go, sir?" I ask the man.

"Uh, it's to go."

"Okay."

"Can I get extra napkins?" he asks.

"Yes."

"Can I get two forks?"

"Yes."

"Can I get, uh, those, um… spoons, too?" The man makes a digging motion with his hand and shovels imaginary food into his mouth.

"Yes. I'll take care of everything, sir. Don't you worry. Twenty-six ninety-eight," I say. I tap the lemon wedge on the register and pull out a large plastic bag from underneath the counter. I give the bag a quick whip in the air. It opens. I put a rubber band around the heavy container. Soy sauce trickles out the edge. The sauce gets on my fingers. I grab a few napkins and wipe my fingers with it after putting the item into the bag. I grab two forks and spoons with my left hand and reach for the napkins with my right. My right hand touches something warm and hairy. I look and the man's hairy hand is already grabbing three inches of napkins and shoving them into his pocket.

"Okay," I say. "Thank you."

"Thanks a lot, miss." He gives me a little wave in the air.

29

Tapes

The tall, skinny black guy with the dreadlocks down to his waist walks in. This is Donald. I once asked him about his dreadlocks. He said it had something to do with his beliefs and that he's had it for eighteen years.

"I'm never going to cut it," he said. "I'm going to grow it till the day I die."

Donald's been working at Hotel Pennsylvania and coming to the deli for breakfast and lunch for fifteen years. He returns in the afternoon for a container of fruit. He always has a pop quiz for me.

"Lemme ask you something since you look educated."

"Fine."

"Federal Reserve. Is it part of the government?"

"Well, it's federal, so I guess it is," I say.

Donald shakes his head and laughs.

"See, I thought you might know but you're not political."

"You're right. I hate politics. It's ruining this country and the rest of the world."

He continues to shake his head and walks to the deli glass and talks to Jose.

A black woman brings two sandwiches to the register with her two young sons. One of the kids brings over a Twix candy bar.

"Oh my god," the woman cries. "Uh-uh. Put it back."

The kid whines.

"Ugh! How much is this?" she asks me.

"It's a dollar twenty-five, but just give me a dollar."

"Jesus! Lord, thank you!" the woman says. She and her two children leave.

Donald brings two bananas to the register and asks me, "You know what turns bananas brown?"

"I don't know. Oxygen?"

He shakes his head.

"Melanin," he says. "I wish I had as much melanin as that woman just now." He shakes his head and walks out the door.

"Watch out for him," says Arnold.

"Huh?"

"He's really into outer space kind of stuff. He gave me a tape," he says.

"What kind of tape?"

"You know…a tape. Like a video. With stuff about life on other planets and shit. I have like five of 'em," Arnold says. "I still have them at home. I'm probably not gonna watch 'em, but they're there," he says.

30

Go

During my residency in Seoul, I was introduced to a novelist known for his erotic story telling named Go—a small, frail looking man with a puffy face. He has a loud voice, and chain-smokes like a fiend. Back in the eighties, he adapted his novel into a screenplay. The story is about a professor having an affair with a former student of his. It did modestly in theaters back then but is now heralded as a classic.

Go teaches creative writing at Ewha Woman's University. He says one of the lessons he teaches the aspiring writers in his class is simply pulling the headphones out of the girls' ears when they're sitting at their desks. He tells them not to walk around while listening to music because it distorts their perception of the world. It winds up connecting the emotions provoked by music to the things they see through their eyes. The world's frankness disappears—only a dishonest association of their musically triggered emotion with what they see out there remains—a romanticized illusion which he considers dangerous.

Go said to me very irritably that portable music is by far the worst thing that was ever invented because it gets in the way of staying grounded to reality. His reality was a harsh one—a sad, hopeless world and so the only escape was through literature injected with some absurdity, humor and eroticism. In Kim

Tongin's stories there is confusion, defeat and death, he said; in Kim Ki-duk's films there is confusion, oppression, defeat and death; in pansori, there is the sound, the deep, guttural wailing that releases bloody sounds into the air. Koreans call it 'han'—a birthmark that is on every Korean. These are the things, said Go, that the students today are letting go of.

"That is tragic to me."

"The young folks today were raised on stupid fads and dramas. They watch TV, get manipulated by all the crying and sappy bullshit that goes on between these actors who don't even have their own real faces anymore, and then they hear whatever music they play fifty million times on the show to really get them hooked. Then what happens? They become addicted to sheer garbage. The manipulative, dramatic music, the accessorized romance of the TV shows, the waste of time. It's like they want to become stupid and stay stupid."

Go shook his head in disgust as he lit another cigarette.

"It's hopeless," he said.

I changed the subject.

"What do your children do?"

"I have a son and a daughter—twins. They both graduated Seoul National University two years ago and they're both unemployed. They live with me and my wife. They're pathetic. I don't know what to do with them."

I didn't say anything. I poured more soju into his glass with two hands.

"You kids in America move out as soon as you graduate college, right?" he asked.

"Not necessarily. Not these days, anyway. We're all readymades. When the economy's bad, it's riskier to live independently, although all of us want to."

Go nodded his head.

"You can't blame your children for what they can't help," I said.

31

Fight

A young black man in a blue button down shirt and a black leather band wristwatch brings a strawberry Dannon yogurt cup to the register.

"Dollar seventy-five," I say.

He hands me his Chase credit card. I hold the card in the air.

"Do you have cash?"

"No."

"There's a five dollar minimum here, sir," I say.

"Whatever. Just swipe it for me."

"I can't do that."

"I come here like everyday. Just swipe it," he says, voice rising.

"Then you should know the rules here."

He lets out an angry puff, and grins at the air. He turns back to me.

"Are you kidding me?"

"No, I'm not."

Arnold walks over to me and says,

"Just swipe it for him. It's okay."

"Thank you, my man," the man tells Arnold. "See? You not in charge. *He* in charge. I come here everyday. Nobody gives me any problems except you."

"Well, I'm working the register today and I'm just doing my job, alright?"

"No. No. You're tripping—that's what you're doing."

I swipe the card, pull out the receipt, and hand him a pen. He signs and throws the receipt and pen towards my direction. The pen bounces off the register and falls behind the cookies. The receipt flies in the air for a second and lands on the scale.

"Don't throw shit at me, motherfucker."

"Dumb bitch." He walks out.

"Dumb bitch, your *mom*!" I yell.

"Fuck you."

"Fuck your mom."

Arnold walks up to me.

"You okay?" he asks.

"Yeah, I'm good."

"What happened?"

"I told the guy that there's a minimum here for credit cards and he didn't want to hear it. Why do I know the rules on credit card minimums here? I'm just doing my job."

"That guy comes in here a lot. Which is why I was wonderin'."

"Well, then he should know better."

I lean against the wooden shelf behind me. The wood feels warm. I've never been able to shake off good or bad feelings very easily before. If something struck me as funny, I laughed at it intensely for long spells of time. If something made me angry or depressed, those sessions carried on for months. I always had trouble getting back to a neutral state. But working at a register changed that. People enter and leave very quickly, so I let my good or bad feelings enter and leave just as quickly as like they do. On average, I meet and greet about sixteen hundred heads in twelve hours. On average, my encounter with every customer lasts between twenty-five to forty-five seconds.

A twenty-something year old blonde white guy brings a half-sandwich wrapped in wax paper with no price marked on it.

"Four ninety-five, on sale, no tax," Arnold says to me.

"Thank you," I say. "Four ninety-five," I tell the kid.

The kid hands me a five.

"Keep the change," he says, reaching over the counter to grab a few napkins. He puts them on top of his sandwich and walks out.

"Thank you." I open the register, pull out a nickel and toss it into a Styrofoam cup.

"Listen," Arnold says. "You like sneakers?"

"What? Why?"

"Well, I get a twenty percent discount on all sneakers at Foot Locker. That kid there works at Foot Locker. So if you ever want some, you let me know."

"Sure thing, Arnold."

"Sometimes, usually in the fall, they have this big sale. And if you go in at the right time, the kid gives me employee discounts."

"Nice."

"Yeah. So you let me know your size, and I'll get you sneakers."

"Okay, Arnold."

32

Pablo

Meeja starts prepping to make yogurt parfaits. She sets out the cutting board, knife, and three bowls, each containing kiwi, strawberry, and pineapple pieces.

A round Latino man wearing a white button-down shirt, blue jeans and brown cowboy boots enters the store. He gives me a small wave with his left hand.

"Hi," he says sweetly.

"Hola, Pablo."

Pablo is Mexican, and he always walks around showing his teeth in a constant grin. He has a big face. His giant nose is a hill situated right below his two large eyes. His eyes look like tortoise shells. His hair is very long and he ties it into a small ponytail that trails down his back.

Pablo walks over to the salad bar.

"Hey, ahjoomah," I say.

"Uh?" Meeja says.

"You know what that guy's name is?"

"Who?"

"That guy with the la guitara," I say, pointing at Pablo. Meeja looks at Pablo pile yellow rice into a plastic container. Meeja looks back down and cuts kiwis into tiny squares.

"That's Pablo. He plays guitar on the seven train and sings," I say.

"He must make a lot of money."

"Yeah?"

"Yeah. I see him come in three to four times a day. He always has a beer." Meeja puts a chunk of kiwi into her mouth and chews. She takes the kiwi squares and drops them into a bowl then begins to cut the strawberries into small squares.

"Yeah. I should quit this job and learn the guitar and go sing on the seven train. I'll sing Cat Power covers."

"Who is Cat Power?"

"She's a singer."

"Okay," Meeja says. "Go do it." Pablo walks over to the register.

"Hi," says Pablo.

"Pa-a-a-a-a-ab-lo," I sing.

"¿Cómo estás?"

"Good. Where's your beer?"

"Aquí." Pablo raises a can of Budweiser, giving me that teeth-grin.

I ring up the items without pushing the tax button. Pablo hands me a ten. I return his change. I place the container onto an orange tray, lay out a napkin and place a fork, knife with the edge turned towards the fork, and finally a spoon.

"Gracias." Pablo takes his tray with two hands and walks to the back of the store.

"Can I bring you anything?" I ask Meeja.

"Go get Pedro to bring more yogurt."

"Okay."

I walk to the back of the store. Pedro is wiping down the orange trays with a white rag. He places the clean ones on top of the garbage disposal box.

"Pedro," I say.

"Si, mi amor."

"Can we get some yogurt when you get a chance? We're making parfaits," I say.

"Okay."

Pedro puts the white rag into his pocket and walks downstairs to the kitchen. I return to the register.

"Pedro is bringing the yogurt," I tell Meeja. I tap my fingers on the register.

"Want me to bring granola?" I ask.

"It's okay. I have." Meeja shakes the plastic bag full of granola.

"Oh."

Pedro returns with six large containers of yogurt.

"Put them here," Meeja says, tapping on the wooden ledge. Pedro sets down the yogurt, one by one, and walks away.

"Thank you, Pedro," I say.

"De nada."

Pedro is always moving around the deli too quickly for me to make small talk with him. I wonder if he has any kids. He's very pale and skinny. He has a thin mustache above his lip. He's always looking down at the ground when he brings the orange plastic trays over to register after he cleans them. I wonder what he thinks about when he gets bored by the trash bin, wiping down a million orange trays.

Pablo reappears again. He stands in front of the register and swings his guitar over to the front.

"I sing for you," Pablo says. He steps back, facing me and Meeja. Meeja continues to cut fruit into small squares, not looking up.

Pablo plucks the strings of the guitar, opening with four notes. His face looks different from before. Each chord makes the inside of the store feel a little different. The colors on the candy wrappers seem brighter and livelier. I turn to Jose. He is nodding his head. He notices me looking at him and laughs. He points to Pablo with his rubber-gloved hand. Arnold returns to the deli platform from his break.

"Oh, he's finally playing for you?" he asks me.

Pablo starts a waltz-like rhythm and begins to sing. I now understand why his voice always sounded so sweet whenever he greeted me. Pablo has a perfect singing voice. He sings in Spanish. I only pick up two words—canto and mano—and forget the rest.

While Pablo sings, people continue to go in and out of the store. Most of them don't look at him. A black woman with bangs, red lipstick and glasses comes in and looks at me. She rolls her eyes and walks over to the salad bar. Pablo finishes. I clap.

"Bravo."

Pablo swings his guitar behind his back and stands there for a moment. Then he raises his hand in the air and waves.

"Okay, bye," he says. Pablo walks out.

"He's so cute!" Gelato Girl says to me. I ignore her and turn to Meeja.

"What did you think of that, ahjoomah?"

"Good." Meeja scoops a spoonful of squared fruit onto a bed of granola over the yogurt.

"Canto and mano," I say. Jose looks at me.

"Canto!" I shout.

"Sing," he replies.

"Mano!"
"Hand."

33

Rafael

An old man with two lazy eyes walks in with his cheeks drooping down like a bulldog's face. He's wearing a tan suit and a brown fedora hat with brown leather shoes to match. He turns and waves at me as he shuffles in.

"Hello, sweetie," he says.

"Hi, Rafael."

Rafael made me guess his age last week. I lied and said he looked sixty-five.

He corrected me and said, "I am eighty-six years old. Do you know why I am still alive and healthy?"

"No."

Rafael leaned in and whispered, "Because I believe in God too much."

"I see."

"If you believe in God, you'll live like I do," he said.

Rafael is a retired music teacher. He taught piano and guitar all his life. He used to be a musician back in the Dominican Republic, which is where he was born. He played most of his music in Puerto Rico for fifteen years before moving to New York in 1960. He comes to the deli every weekend to eat chicken, rice and seafood salad upstairs in the seating area. He always takes lemon slices and extra packets of salt, and he is always alone.

Rafael carries over a large plastic container of steamed salmon, tuna salad, roasted eggplant and yellow rice.

"You should learn to play the guitar," he says.

"Should I?"

"Yes. Twenty dollars a lesson, once a week. I will teach you a method. You buy a book, and practice this method. And you will play very well. You're at a good age for it."

"I don't know if that's true anymore."

"No, no. You are at a good age for this. Listen, go to Forty-fourth Street, between Eighth and Ninth Avenue. Do you know this place?"

"I think I can find it."

"Go there, and ask for the cheapest guitar, and they will give you something. Try it out."

"Okay."

"Think it over."

Rafael pays for his food then carries the tray over to the fridge. Meeja takes a few lemon slices from a container by the yogurt cups and places them on a napkin for him on his tray.

"Bye, LJ," he says, smiling at me. I smile back and watch him carry the tray upstairs to the dining area.

34

Trays

The one object that reduces a person's overall appearance to awkward, stupid and herd-like is the tray. Ever since I was a child, I hated them. At cafeteria lines in schools and summer camps, I always refused to collect a tray. For me, it was bad enough that I had to physically move about the cafeteria in a systemic manner, standing in line after line for each food category—salad, prepped and processed entrées, dessert, sugary drink selections of iced tea, lemonade and sodas. I couldn't understand the shamelessness of my peers who stood about in lines with a big plastic tray in hideous colors like brown and orange, their steel utensils sliding around noisily over the pebbled surface, waiting for servers with hair nets and gloves behind counters to scoop and drop the foods in large chunks from stainless steel bins and onto their plates. They looked stupid, and so did I. It looked and felt stupid to move so systematically with so many various functions only to fulfill such a basic need—hunger. Anyway, trays are awful.

Standing by a register and selling food all day, I eventually start to see the people as the stuff they eat. The people carry trays with Styrofoam containers full of greasy food and sauces loaded with artificial flavoring and chemicals that eventually turn into their flesh, bones and hair. The people who come to the deli may come from different places and different parents, but they are all eating the same stuff that eventually turn into a part of their physical makeup or turn into waste. They all become the same by being partially made up of the same substances, and suddenly the cultural, educational, class and race gaps are no longer there. I just see the people who come and eat the food purchased from a deli as lumps of flesh. As thousands of people flow into the deli in a matter of hours that I am there, at some point during the day, I momentarily lose track of their distinctions. When they walk in, they're different but once they leave, they leave with the same kinds of food in their guts.

The genius of the tray is that it is a great way to make money. At the deli, a place where everything costs too much money, and where food taken from steam tables and salad bars are charged by the pound, trays are moneymaking tools. The saying that one should not go food shopping when one is hungry applies here at the deli; one should not go into a deli and pick up a tray when hungry. Humans are not too complicated in their thinking sometimes. For example, in recent years, universities have been eliminating trays from the cafeterias because studies show that trays facilitate gluttony. When a person is given a tray, the person sees a blank space that simply needs to be filled. If the person is hungry, that space will likely be filled with a lot more than what the person can actually handle. The automatic task assigned to that person at that point is to fill that space with food. In a place like the deli or a cafeteria, the tray will be carried around until the tray's surface area is completely filled. This is the natural way that an unthinking person behaves when that person is motivated by hunger.

At a cafeteria, when a tray's surface area is full, it means that the person is purchasing more food items. Whether or not the person will be able to finish eating everything that is on the tray is not the cafeteria's concern. Chances are, that person will not be able to. If the person does finish all the items on that tray, chances are, that that person's risk of obesity and heart related diseases will increase. This is why some universities in the US are now abandoning trays completely.

The deli offers trays. To be honest, I really don't see the need for them a lot of the times. Trays only inconvenience people here at the deli. For instance, bottled waters or sodas always tip over when patrons try to pick up the tray from the stack of other trays below it. If that's the case, the patron is just better off taking the Styrofoam container of food in one hand and the bottled soda in the other, but since a tray is there, they will always take it. Furthermore, the trays at this deli are not to be used or trusted. People come in here and grab trays without thinking then walk over to the deli counter to request sandwiches, or they take them to the steam tables or the salad bar to fill up their Styrofoam or plastic containers full of food. Then they place their utensils and napkins directly onto the tray, carry it to their seat to eat and afterwards, it is taken to the garbage receptacle, where it gets pushed into the swinging garbage dispenser door then pulled back out after it is emptied of its contents. Then it gets placed on top of the garbage receptacle, along with the other trays that have been inserted into the trash bin then removed. These trays have been touched by thousands of hands. Pedro takes the rag that hangs out of his back pocket and wipes the tray down once, using the same rag for all the trays and all the counters of the deli and brings them over to the register counter where they get placed to my left in two neat piles beside the scale and register. The unassuming next patron grabs the tray and eats from it without thinking twice about where it has been (inside the garbage can) and who and what has touched it.

"Jose, do these trays get washed at the end of the day?"

"No."

"When do they get washed?"

"Maybe twice a week."

"Oh my god…"

Jose laughs.

A man walks up and places his sixteen-ounce coffee on the tray and picks it up. As he turns, he pauses and sneezes. The coffee shakes and spills all over the tray. The man looks at me and hands me the tray and partially full coffee cup. I take it and toss the coffee into the trash bin. I hand the tray to Pedro who wipes it down with the same rag. I watch as the man walks over to the coffee dispenser and refills a fresh cup.

35

Hot Water

A Chinese man drags in a luggage on wheels, carrying a hot thermos.

"Hot wata?" he asks.

I nod my head at him. He smiles and drags his luggage to the coffee dispenser counter and fills his thermos. Meeja looks up at him then turns to me.

"Charge him one dollar," she says to me in Korean. As the man turns back around I call out after him, "One dollar." The man freezes and gives me an exasperated look.

"One dolla for this much wata?!" and makes a small invisible box the size of Tic-Tacs with his two fingers.

"Yes."

"One dolla for this much wata!" he screams again. He looks at me with disgust. The ice cream man, Oskar, walks in with his thermos. He raises it at me and I nod. Oskar fills his thermos full of hot water from the dispenser then leaves the store waving at me. The man drops his jaw at the sight then points at Oskar's back, shouting, "You let him take! Why not I take?!"

"Sir, that man stands inside an air-conditioned ice cream truck all day in shorts. And he gives me ice cream whenever I say 'hi' to him. Of course he takes!" The man is not listening. He's still screaming over my sentences,

"One dolla for this much wata!" He drags his black luggage behind him as he leaves the store, shouting things into the air. He continues down the street like that for another five seconds until he disappears from my sight completely.

36

The Ice Cream Man

I remember the first time I met Oskar. I was in a good mood that day. When he came up to me, I immediately liked his hat, his white hair, beard, and his very round, alert blue eyes that fell slightly at the ends of each corner. I liked the way he spoke—how considerate he was of each word he delivered in his German accent.

He asked me, "May I take some hot water?"

"Go ahead." Oskar took his hot water then returned to the register.

"Do you like ice cream?" he asked. I grinned.

"I sell this product. It has been in this city for many decades. It is low in fat and very delicious. This product is called Tasti D-Lite." We've been friends ever since.

Oskar returns to the store and walks up to the register.

"Hey Oskar."

"Business is slow," he says.

"It'll pick up soon."

"Yes. There is an event happening around the corner."

"Really?"

"Yes. A fashion show."

"When do you stop driving the truck?"

"October."

"What will you do in the winter?"

"Nothing."

"No work?"

"I must recharge."

"Yeah," I say. "I hear that."

He looks down at the caramel peanut bars, the cookie packages containing four macadamia nut and cranberry cookies, 5-Hour Energy drinks, and ginseng liquid shots.

"Where in Germany are you from?"

"North," he says. "Very cold."

"East or West?"

"West." He lowers his head slightly with his eyes fixated on mine. "But it is still one country. It was divided only for a short period."

"Uh-huh."

"Divided thanks to the Americans and British." Oskar stares at the cookies and the energy drinks again then raises his head.

"Like how Korea's been divided thanks to the Russians and the Americans," I say. "For sixty years now. Or rather, just differences in ideology."

"Is there light at the end of the tunnel?"

"No."

"When do you think there will be?"

"Maybe never," I said. "Maybe if Kim Jong-il dies and his successor applies his European education towards something good for his people. Maybe then people can look around for some light. I'm not looking though."

"When I look at the leader of this country on the television, he always looks like Mao to me," Oskar says.

"I guess he does kind of resemble him."

"Yes. There is no sign of intelligence coming from this man's appearance. He looks," Oskar brings his hand to his head and shakes it a little bit, "off in the head. Like he is not all there."

"North Korea's leader is not playing with a full deck."

"How many people live under this man's leadership?"

"I'm not sure. Maybe something like twenty million," I said. "I don't really know, to be honest."

"The Americans and the British were bombing all over Germany. Like they bombed Japan," Oskar says.

"The Americans later bombed North Korean civilians with a technology that they'd learned from the Japanese," I say. "It involved dropping little canisters of insects that carried diseases. North Koreans harbor a lot of bad feelings toward America and Japan," I say.

"It's all about global power."

"Why do the UK and America always get involved in other people's business?" I ask.

"Because people want to get paid," Oskar says.

"Do you know how much the US government makes from their military bases in Korea alone?" I ask.

"How much?"

"Billions," I say. "Through black markets that sell guns, cigarettes—all kinds of US products that are made in China. They profit off of prostitution, too. People think that we're spending too many tax dollars by getting involved in other countries' affairs but what they don't recognize is just how much money the US is making after they set up military bases in those countries. Look at Afghanistan. Look at Iraq. Look at Guam. Look at Japan. Look at Korea. The US is never going to leave. The US has been in Korea for sixty years. You can see kids trick-or-treating nowadays in Seoul. If people think that South Korea is an independent country, they need to think again."

"It all seems like a conspiracy," Oskar says.

"Culture is a scam," I say.

Oskar looks down at the cookies again sadly.

A blonde girl brings over a package of cookies and chips to the register. She hands me a twenty. I ring her up.

"During the second World War, I was still a child, but I remember American airplanes flying very low over our heads. I was walking home from school, and as they were flying overhead, they were shooting at us. Even now, I think about it and my skin rises." Oskar points to his arm.

"War is a fight for global power. The French, the British, the Americans…they always picked on us. They forget that it was the Germans who built the printing press six hundred years ago. Without it, there would be no newspaper, no internet, no media," Oskar says.

"The world would be a better place without the media. We are all constructed from culture and history that have nothing to do with us."

"The word 'delicatessen' is a German word. I don't know if you knew that," Oskar says.

He stares at the pills again. I stare at the register. The blonde girl waits for her change. I hand her the change. She asks me for a bag. I throw a bag at her and it falls onto the sliding glass door of the freezer. She takes it and walks out of the store, glaring at me.

"War is just a game for corporations and the government.

But for the small person like you and me, it is just something on the news," Oskar says. He turns and exits the store.

37

Thoreau

I lean my head back, against the cigarettes. I turn around and touch the row of Benson & Hedges. Then I slide my hand down the row of American Spirits. These two brands of cigarettes cost fourteen dollars a box. The rest cost thirteen. Each pack has a small pink label pasted onto them that reads, "New York City." The labels are there to prove that the city's cigarette taxes have been paid for. I look at the green row of Salems, the blue and brown cartons of Camels, and the silver, gold, green and red cartons of Marlboros. Marlboro reds are very popular among European tourists.

I stand up straight and see a small bearded white man standing in front of me with a bottle of Samuel Adams Summer Ale.

"How you doing, sir," I say.

"Okay, thanks." He has small wrinkles around his eyes. He probably has a sweet smile. He's wearing a shirt with some quote by Thoreau but I don't have enough time to read the whole thing.

"Was Thoreau a good man?" I ask.

"Um. I'd like to think so..." he says, smiling. The wrinkles around his eyes deepen.

"Okay." I uncap his beer with the bottle opener.

"Okay. Two fifty," I say. I put two napkins down and hand

him the beer. The bearded white man hands me three singles in return.

"I see you around Borders a lot," he says.

"Yeah. I like it in there."

The bearded man takes his beer and raises it at me. He walks to the back of the store towards the seating area. He has a small book tucked under his arm. I want to ask him what he's reading. I'd forgotten to ask.

My back aches. I shut my eyes again.

"Hello?"

I open my eyes.

A Latino man with a mustache is standing there in a blue button down shirt and navy blue slacks. There's a set of keys dangling from a belt loop.

"Sorry," I say.

"It's okay. I've had those moments." He places a Styrofoam container on the scale. It weighs over three pounds.

"Twenty-three eighteen," I say.

"Jesus. That much?"

"Yeah. Sorry."

"It's alright. Can I get a bag?"

"Sure."

I put a rubber band around the container then put it into a large plastic bag along with napkins, a fork and a knife.

"May I get a spoon, too, please?"

"Sure."

I tie the bag into a knot and hand it to him. I yank on the merchant's receipt from the card machine.

"Need a receipt?"

"No, thanks."

"Sign please."

He signs and hands me the receipt. He's written "2.00" on the tip line.

"Thanks," I say.

"Thank you, now. Bye." He breezes out the door. It's very bright out. A warm afternoon glow covers everything outside. The people on Seventh Avenue are walking more slowly than they did earlier.

"Cuantos ahoras, Jose?"

"Tres ahoras," he says. I give him a thumbs-up. He chuckles.

"Cansado," I say.

38

Hapcheon II

LJ and Daniel rode the small green village bus along with two elderly women and an elderly man. The man wore a straw hat. The two women wore visors. The bus made its way through an elevated path. Below the path were large fields of cabbage, onions, carrots, and spinach. LJ pointed at orange-netted sacks full of onions placed randomly throughout the field.

"Look," she said, "they grow like that. In orange sacks like that just naturally."

"Really?"

"No."

Daniel smirked.

"Should we bring anything to your grandparents?"

"Maybe just some food. There's a market just outside of the village gate. We'll stop by."

Daniel pointed at the roofs of the houses they passed.

"Those look interesting. All roofs should look like that," Daniel said.

"They're cooked in fire. They're called 'giwa.' I think the Dutch have a similar kind of roof, except theirs is orange, not dark blue."

"That's black, not blue," Daniel said.

"Whatever. Dark blue."

"Black."

LJ and Daniel got off at Ssang-baek village. They stopped by at a butcher and got four servings of pork belly then picked up makkeolli and beers from a deli next door.

"Do we need any lettuce leaves or garlic?"

"No," LJ said. "We'll just get it from my grandparents' garden."

"Nice."

LJ and Daniel walked across a small bridge suspended over a creek.

"LJ, can I walk down there?"

Daniel pointed at the shallow creek and giants slabs of flat stones.

"If you want. Careful of snakes."

"Snakes?"

"In the grass. Yeah."

"Okay. Come with me."

Daniel took LJ's hand and eased them both down to the bottom of the hill. Daniel stood in the shallow end of the creek and stared at the rushing water just a few feet away from him and LJ.

"Okay, c'mon. Let's go. My grandmother's gonna meet us out front."

"Okay."

"We'll come back tomorrow."

LJ and Daniel emerged from the hill. Up ahead, LJ spotted her grandmother coming towards them on a scooter.

"Is this the guy you're going to marry?" LJ's grandmother asked as she motored her way through the narrow path of the village towards the house.

"No. We're friends."

"Hm. He speaks Korean?"

"Yes," Daniel answered in Korean.

"Hm. How long are you going to stay?"

"Just one night, halmeoni."

"We'll stop at the house, drop off your things then go to the field."

LJ and Daniel followed LJ's grandmother towards the house. They pushed open through a large blue gate. A yard of concrete pavement appeared. To the right was a small stable with a cow and her calf, and stacks of hay beside them. To the left was a water pump, a couple of machinery and a storage compartment built from beams of wood. Hanging from the ceiling of the compartment were bunches of garlic.

LJ's grandfather stepped out of the house.

"Harabeoji!" LJ cried.

"Why are you back already?" he asked.

"What are you talking about? I haven't seen you in months."

"When do you go back to America?"

"Next week."

"Okay. You staying the night?"

"Yes."

"Hm."

Daniel bowed.

"Who is that?" LJ's grandfather asked.

"That's Daniel. He's my friend."

"Are you getting married to that guy?"

"No."

"Hm."

LJ and Daniel watched LJ's grandfather walk over to the

stacks of hay, slightly hunched over in his black trousers and a white T-shirt. He reached for an armful of hay and dropped it into the trough in front of the cow. The cow immediately went for it.

LJ's grandmother walked out from behind the house where she parked her scooter. She carried a red plastic bowl containing two small knives.

"Let's go get some greens," she said.

"Halmeoni, when are you going to sell the cow?"

"Not sure. We sold a calf last year. Got two million *won* for it."

"Wow."

LJ's grandmother led them out the gate and through a narrow path. To the left was a large rice field. Far up ahead were mountains. They had fuzzy yellow patches around the middle.

"What is that?" Daniel asked.

"Those are chestnut trees."

"Wow."

"Yeah. We pick chestnuts in the fall. They come in these huge spiky balls. We pick them up off the ground, break it open with our feet and take the chestnuts from the inside. We wear these thick gloves when we do it."

"Sounds dangerous," Daniel said.

"It is. It's fun, too. My harabeoji takes this huge bamboo stalk and whacks the trees so the chestnuts fall to the ground. And halmeoni picks them up. My aunts and uncles and cousins come every season to help."

They walked by a stable full of cows. The cows mooed loudly.

"Halmeoni, why do they keep mooing?" LJ asked. "It's so annoying."

"Cows have a right to their own song," LJ's grandmother replied.

"You're right," Daniel said to LJ's grandmother.

"Your Korean's good," LJ's grandmother said.

"Thank you."

"How long have you been here?"

"A year and a half."

"Are you going back to America with LJ?"

"She leaves soon but I'm staying in Seoul for another six months."

Past the stables was a garden with red leaf lettuce, radishes and eggplants. LJ's grandmother handed LJ and Daniel each a knife.

"Cut the lettuce leaves right above the root. One clean cut," LJ's grandmother instructed.

"Okay."

LJ's grandmother walked towards the concrete wall that separated the lettuce garden from the stables. She pulled a large machete from behind a shrub with small red berries. She walked over to a large bamboo stalk and reached for the highest part in her reach. She gave the bamboo stalk several hard whacks until it broke off.

"Here," she said as she dragged it towards Daniel. "Go fishing with LJ later."

"Thanks."

LJ's grandmother reached for a smaller stalk that looked like a cone wrapped in purple and brown leaves. She gave it a swift whack with the machete and it came clean off straight into her hand.

"What is that, halmeoni?"

"This is a baby bamboo. The inside is edible."

"Really?"

"Of course."

LJ's grandmother handed the baby stalk to Daniel.

"Halmeoni, what are those berries?"

"These?"

LJ's grandmother picked a few berries and handed them to LJ.

"These are edible," she said. LJ handed a couple to Daniel, who threw them straight into his mouth. He nodded. The three of them returned to the house.

LJ and her grandmother drew water into a large silver basin in the yard. Daniel grabbed his camera and photographed the two women wash the dirt off the greens. LJ's grandmother stripped the leaves off the baby bamboo stalk. A bright green inside revealed itself. LJ's grandmother ran a knife through it length-wise. Inside was a dozen small compartments.

"Daniel, look. It looks like an apartment," LJ said.

"You boil this, then add seasoning. Some sesame oil, garlic, soy sauce and red pepper flakes, and you have a side dish."

"Can we eat it raw?" Daniel asked.

LJ's grandmother broke off a piece and handed it to him.

LJ watched Daniel pop it into his mouth. He made a face.

"Oh my god. That was not a good idea," he said.

LJ's grandmother laughed.

"What time should we have dinner?" LJ asked.

"Whenever you want."

"Couple of hours? We'll go for a walk around town."

"Okay. Harabeoji will have the grill ready for you."

39

Arnold

A twenty-something year old white guy asks Arnold for a ham and cheese.

"On what?" Arnold asks.

"Long roll."

"Hah?"

"Long roll," the guy repeats.

"You want lettuce, tomato?"

"Yes."

"You want mayo-mustard-honeymustard-oil-and-vinegar-thousandisland-chipotle-or-mustard?"

"Um… mustard," the guy says.

Arnold nods his head once. He goes to the deli glass, pulls out a block of Boar's Head ham and takes it to the meat slicer. He smiles at me.

"I want Katz pastrami," I say.

"On Houston?"

"Yeah."

"I used to live there."

"Yeah?"

"Yeah. Lower East Side. Lived there my whole life."

Arnold is almost sixty years old. He has three grown daughters who are all married, and a thirty-year-old son who lives alone in the Bronx. Arnold told me that he still supports his son financially because the boy has "mental problems." Arnold works seven days a week to get by—just like me.

"I pay his five hundred dollar rent every month. That's why I gotta work seven days a week."

Arnold is Puerto Rican. He was born at Bellevue Hospital and grew up in the Lower East Side. He now lives in Jackson Heights with his second wife. He used to roll with a gang that called themselves the Dynamite Brothers back in the 70s.

"I did every kind of drug back then. I used to have that big Afro, poppin' uppers and downers, snortin' all kinds of shit, you know…" Arnold moves his hands around a lot when he tells me stories. He wears a small paper hat on his bald head. He sticks his neck out a little bit whenever he speaks and his head bobs slightly with the movement of his hands whenever he pauses for emphasis or a reaction from me. He has a big belly and pale, skinny legs.

"But I never touched the needle," he says. "I did everything but the needle, and when I say everything, I mean *everything*."

Arnold wraps up the sandwich in wax paper and hands it me.

"Six ninety-five," he says. I raise the sandwich in the air and the guy walks over to the register. He pays for it in cash.

"Bag?" I say.

"No, it's fine. Thanks."

I hand him a few napkins and turn back to Arnold.

"Growin' up in the Lower East Side, we had gangs but it was to protect our families, you know?"

"Sure."

"It was dangerous back then. I mean, I seen some shit. You go upstairs into a building and there were crack heads crawling around the staircases lookin' all over the ground for a small white pebble. Then one day, I find myself on the floor, lookin' for that same fuckin' pebble so I said, nope. Can't do this anymore. So I got cleaned up, quit drugs. I was in and out of jails for doin' crazy shit, and my first wife left me when I was twenty-two. So I went to church and put it all down before god. I said, 'God. Help me.' And didn't go back to drugs. Met my wife today. My wife's Irish. My son has red hair."

Arnold reaches into his back pocket and opens his wallet. He shows me a picture of his son. I see a good-looking kid with wavy red hair, a big grin and dark eyes.

Everything that Arnold says sounds like a line from a movie. He speaks the way characters do in films like *Carlito's Way* or *Dog Day Afternoon*. His stories are full of so many climactic elements. I don't know if he does it just to attention grab or if the way he speaks is the reason why people make films about New York.

Meeja walks over and tells us to break it up. A tall old white man with hunched shoulders wobbles in with a suitcase, a plaid suit, and brown slacks. He has a few wisps of gray hair covering a large bald spot on his head. He's frowning and his body is shaking. He goes to the fridge and brings a can of Sprite to the register.

"Dollar twenty-five," I say.

"Napkins," he says.

I take a few napkins and place them on top of the can. The man's hands shake as he hands me the money. They sway left and right. He has Parkinson's disease. The man takes the can and goes outside. He stands by the trash bin, cracks the can open and drinks from it. I realize then why he asked for napkins for his soda: His hands shake so badly that he spills soda all over his shirt and his hands. I watch him finish drinking the soda and throw the empty can into the bin. He disappears down south. I really want to ask him what he does for a living and where he works. He usually comes in about three to four times a day and always buys a can of Sprite. He never buys anything to eat.

Meeja walks to the back of the store. Arnold comes and stands beside me again.

"When we were kids, we played handball at our school yard. There was this guy, we called him 'Chino.' He was half Chinese, half Puerto Rican. He had a really good arm."

"Wow."

"Hey, you know Hell's Angels?"

"Yeah."

"They used to be in my neighborhood," he says.

"I think they're still in the Lower East Side," I say.

"We knew this one guy. We called him Short Eye. He got into a bar fight with one of those guys once. Son of a bitch got his ass *beat*." Arnold punches his palm for emphasis.

"Excuse me, miss?" a middle-aged black woman asks.

"Yes?"

"Do you have pound cake?"

"No, ma'am. Sorry."

"Oh… you don't have pound cake?"

"No." I look down at my watch then back up at her.

"We have muffins and candy bars," I tell her.

"No… I want something like a pound cake… something really sweet."

"We have chocolate muffins."

"Mm…" The woman stands there, pouting.

A tall Italian man with a red, white and green t-shirt walks around the woman and up to the register. He raises a large coffee cup at me then sets it down.

"How much is this?" he asks.

"A dollar seventy five."

"Are you for sale?" he asks.

"No, I am not."

"Okay." He hands me seven quarters.

"Good answer," he says.

"Bye now."

The woman continues to stand there, looking at me. Her eyes are wide open, staring blankly ahead.

"Ma'am, I don't know what to tell you. We don't have pound cakes," I say.

"Okay, okay." She raises her palms in the air. Her fingernails are long and painted red. Arnold steps down from the platform and walks over to an old man getting coffee from the dispensers. He looks to be about Arnold's age, and has a large hump on his back. He has gigantic green eyes and a white cap that says, 'US Open 2006.' He's wearing a green and white striped polo shirt.

Arnold fills a Styrofoam cup with coffee. The man asks Arnold if there's any Splenda. Arnold turns around and reaches for the shelves below the banana basket. He pulls out two packets of Equal and two packs of Sweet 'n' Low.

"Thank you," the man says.

"Ay, where you from?" Arnold asks him.

"I grew up on Long Island."

"You look Puerto Rican."

"My father is Puerto Rican. My mother is Italian."

"I see."

The man brings his small coffee to the register. He walks carefully across the tile floor.

"Dollar twenty-five."

"This and I'm having a buttered bagel."

"Sure thing."

Arnold hands me a bagel wrapped in foil.

"Ninety-five cents, on sale," he says, giving me a wink. I put the bagel into a small brown paper bag with two napkins.

"Two twenty," I say.

The hunched man hands me three singles and I return his change.

"Thanks. Have a good one."

40

Big Phil

"Heeeeeeeeey, Big Philly."

Big Phil smiles at me.

"How are you doing, gorgeous?" Big Phil has a thick baritone voice and a light Trinidadian accent. He has small eyes, a round baldhead, and a massive body. He weighs around three hundred pounds, and works as the security guard next door at the Chinese fast food joint and the Greek gyro place.

"Good. How is security guarding?" I ask.

"You know. All mental."

"Well, you're a big guy so I doubt anybody will hassle you."

"Like I said, it is all mental."

"Ha ha."

"What are you going to do for your weekend?"

"I'm working, baby. I work seven days," I reply.

Big Phil widens his tiny eyes a bit. I feel like laughing. The skin around his eyebrows and forehead tighten and turn a bit lighter in color.

"You work *seven* days?"

"Yes."

"What do you do for fun?"

"This is pretty fun," I say.

"I don't believe you. You're too young."

A Russian man with a beard brings a large Styrofoam container and a bottle of Arizona iced tea, blueberry acai flavored.

"Excuse me," he says. "Is this delicious?" He raises the iced tea in the air.

"I couldn't tell you, boss," I say. "Never tried it." I ring up the items and point to the register screen. The Russian digs for his wallet. He hands me a twenty. After receiving his change, he immediately shakes the iced tea and opens it. He takes a sip, swallows then nods his head, looking at me.

"Is it delicious?" I ask.

"Mm," he says, nodding. He carries his tray to the back.

A short Latino man enters.

"Excuse me!" he says. I look at him.

"Phone card! Do you have!" he shouts.

"Five or ten?" I ask.

"Ehhhhhh. Five."

I turn around, reach for a Boss phone card of five dollars worth and hand it to him. He hands me a five-dollar bill. I put the bill underneath the register where we collect the phone card money.

"Do you have coin?" he asks.

"For what?"

"For cccckkkkkkrrrrrrggghhhhh," he says. The short man makes a rigorous scratching motion across the air.

I reach into my tip cup and hand him a quarter. He scratches the silver layer off the phone card then returns the quarter to me.

"Bye bye!" the man shouts before leaving.

"See ya."

Big Phil heads out the door with a large coffee cup.

"Okay, I'll see you later," Big Phil says, waving at me. I wave back. I look at Meeja walk behind a tall white man with gray hair, a blue button down shirt, and jeans. She's walking very close, practically stepping on his heels.

"Excuse me," Meeja says. The man ignores her. He has a newspaper covering something in his hand.

"Excuse me," she repeats. The man looks behind at her then breaks into a run.

"Ooooorrrrghhh!" The noise comes from Meeja. I look up and see her chasing the man, and she sounds like a gorilla. The man sprints out the door and into the street. Cars are coming but he doesn't look. He runs for it. A cab stops and blares its horn. The man makes it to the other side and disappears around the corner of Bank of America.

"What did he do?" I ask.

"He took food from the salad bar. He covered it with a newspaper."

I laugh at Meeja.

"You can't stop guys like that. When they walk in, they're determined to steal from you. There's just no way to stop them," she says.

Gelato Girl returns from the bathroom.

"What happened?" she asks.

"Somebody stole food," I say.

"Was he black?" Gelato Girl asks.

"What? No. He was white."

"Was he homeless?"

"I don't know. I don't know..."

"Oh. That's weird," she says returning to her post behind the gelato fridge.

41

Brownies

A black girl and her younger sister walk up to the register. The older sister is heavy-set wearing gray sweatpants with a white tank top. The younger sister is very skinny. She talks rapidly, moving her hands a lot while telling her sister a story. The older sister places two small plastic cartons on the scale. One contains bell peppers, feta cheese, red onions, avocadoes and Romaine lettuce; the other has macaroni and cheese, and roast chicken slices with onions.

"Together?" I ask.

"Mm-hm," the older sister says while looking through her wallet.

I ring up the items.

"Ten ninety-one," I say.

The older sister continues to look through her wallet. She eventually hands me two fives and says, "I got change for you," and pulls out a pink change purse.

I hear coins hitting the floor. The younger sister says, "You droppin' brownies everywhere."

"Pick 'em up."

"The brownies?" the younger sister asks.

"Yeah. It adds up." The older sister looks at me and widens her eyes, tilting her head to the side.

I smile then ask, "To go?"

"Yes, ma'am."

I put the containers into a plastic bag and tie the handles into a knot.

"Thank you, ladies," I say. The older sister takes the plastic bag and says, "Thank you." The girls leave.

A middle-aged Latina woman with dyed-red hair and very pale, wrinkly white skin hobbles over to the register.

"Toothpaste?" she asks me.

I don't say anything.

"Wood picks?" she asks.

I turn around and grab three toothpicks from a box. I hand them to her.

"Toothpicks," I say.

"Ah, yes. Thank you. You know." The woman leaves.

42

Hapcheon III

LJ and Daniel grabbed their cameras and walked through town. Cows mooed, roosters crowed.

"There's a puppy at that house there," LJ said.

"Let's go see it."

"They might've eaten it."

"Really?"

"Yeah."

"Oh my god."

"Yeah. They really do that down here. Not so much in the city but here, dogs are medicine. But they might have another puppy."

LJ and Daniel walked down a slight hill and turned left into a neighboring gate.

"Hello?" LJ said. No one responded. Chains rattled. LJ and Daniel saw a small white puppy jumping up, tied to a light chain next to a doghouse. Daniel petted the puppy while LJ photographed the two.

"This thing is so cute. Are they really going to eat it?" Daniel asked.

"They might. They ate the first one. I heard they cooked it up and gave it to their nephew here before he went to serve in the army."

"Wow. This is so depressing."

The puppy licked Daniel's hand.

"Alright, let's go."

LJ photographed a flight of concrete stairs attached to the side of a building that led up to the roof without any handrails.

"Let's shoot from up there."

LJ and Daniel stood on the roof deck and surveyed the landscape. Rice fields dominated the view. Mountains were in the distance. A large creek ran through the outer edge of the town.

"Where does the creek lead to?" Daniel asked.

"A small reservoir. And then the lake further out north."

LJ and Daniel walked down a dirt path that led upwards into a wooden area. They were surrounded by tall bamboo trees. Dead leaves covered the ground beneath them. The sounds of cows and roosters were muffled and distant. The air was slightly humid and the path grew darker. Daniel took LJ's hand and led them deeper into the woods.

"Someone's going to see us," she said.

"Nobody's here. Seriously. How many people live in this town?"

"I don't know. Fourteen maybe."

"That's more than I thought."

"What a place though," said LJ. "I'll bet back in the day, whenever people wanted to have an affair, they came and did it here."

Daniel dragged LJ closer then dropped his arm across her shoulders.

"I came through this path a long time ago when I was a kid. I was like four or five and my grandparents were going into the woods to forage wild mushrooms and ginseng and such.

We went deep into the mountains. Everything was really dark and damp, but there were bright colored bugs everywhere. They were bright blue or bright yellow. It was incredible. But my arms and neck were really itchy when I came back down. I thought I was gonna die."

The bamboo canopy began to dwindle. Up ahead was an exit. The path below them was concrete again. LJ and Daniel walked down the path and made a left onto a ledge. Below the ledge was a canal for water to stream through. The concrete was black with large cracks running through it. The parts of the concrete were covered in mold. In between the cracks were moss.

As they walked closer towards the town, the sound of cows grew louder. They reached the town path again and heard a dog bark. They looked to their right and saw a large boxer standing on his hind legs with his forepaws dangling down in front of him. The dog frowned at them.

A woman walked out wearing a towel around her head. She wore large parachute pants, a red button down cardigan and purple rubber slip-ons. She was carrying a large tin basin full of cabbage.

"Whose kid are you?" she asked LJ.

"Hee-jun's. Park Hee-jun is my mother."

"You're Hee-jun's kid? You've grown. How's your mom? She still in America?"

"Yes."

"You're here to see halmeoni and harabeoji?"

"Yes."

"Who is that?"

"This is Daniel. He's a friend."

Daniel bowed.

"What's he doing here?" the woman asked.

"He's just here to visit my grandparents with me."

"Are you two getting married?"

"No. He's just a friend."

"Even if you're not getting married, I don't like that he's here."

"Alright, ma'am. Have a good night."

"I don't like it. Don't bring them here," she called after LJ.

Back at the house, LJ's grandfather had a large square tin out in the yard. LJ's grandmother had already placed the lettuce on the table set up on the veranda just outside the sliding doors of the hanok bedrooms.

"Daniel, can you help my harabeoji with the fire?"

"Sure."

Daniel approached LJ's grandfather. LJ's grandfather motioned Daniel away. Daniel persisted and took the large block of wood from him. LJ's grandfather offered Daniel a small ax. Daniel broke the wood into small pieces and dropped them into the tin hearth. LJ watched from the veranda while helping her grandmother finish setting up the table.

"There's a stew on the stove," LJ's grandmother said. "Dwen-jang."

"Okay, halmeoni."

"You said you're not going to marry that boy?"

"No. I'm too young to get married. Do you think I should marry him?"

"It's your life. You should marry whoever you like."

"True. Harabeoji would hate it if I married a white guy."

"Do what you want to do. Harabeoji has nothing to do with your decision to marry who you want."

"True."

"Go fishing tomorrow with Daniel. The line and bait are still in the storage room from last time. But catch and release only, okay?"

"Okay halmeoni."

LJ watched Daniel squat over the tin hearth, looking up at LJ's grandfather while he lit a match. Daniel took the dried pine needles on the ground next to him and dropped them into the hearth. LJ's grandfather dropped the match onto the needles.

"Go to the back of the house. Get more of this," LJ's grandfather said. Daniel said,

"Yes," then ran to the back of the house. He returned with a handful of dried leaves and pine needles.

LJ's grandfather placed a metal net over the hearth.

"Where's the meat?"

LJ carried a plate of pork belly over to him with scissors and metal tongs.

"We'll grill the meat, harabeoji."

"No. I'll do it. You'll burn your hands."

At the dinner table, LJ wrapped lettuce leaves with pork belly, garlic cloves, green pepper and dwen-jang. She handed one to her grandfather, then her grandmother and one to Daniel.

"Harabeoji, Daniel ate a raw piece of baby bamboo today."

LJ's grandmother laughed hysterically.

"You shouldn't do that," LJ's grandfather said without looking up from his food.

"It tastes good now, Daniel. Try it," LJ's grandmother said. She took a bit of the seasoned bamboo and placed it onto Daniel's spoon.

"It's good," he said. "You're right."

"You can sleep in this room. I'll share the middle room with my halmeoni. My harabeoji's going to sleep in the room at the farthest end," LJ said.

"Okay."

"By the way, it's important to greet them in the morning, and before retiring in the evening. Before you go to sleep, be sure to tell my grandparents to rest well. And in the morning, be sure to ask if they've had a good rest. Okay?"

"Okay. Can you say the whole sentence in Korean for me again?"

"'Ahn-yeong-hee joo-moo-sae-yo,' for 'good night,' and 'ahn-yeong-hee joo-moo-sheot-seo-yo' in the morning—past tense."

"Ah. Got it. Thanks. Good night, LJ."

"Night."

Early next morning, LJ's grandfather had already headed out to the field to work. LJ's grandmother had a table set up with fried eggs, rice, kimchi and a bowl full of yellow melons.

"Going fishing today?" LJ's grandmother asked.

"Yes. Then the bus straight after."

"Alright."

After breakfast, LJ helped clear the table then did the dishes. LJ's grandmother packed garlic, cucumbers and a small jar of kimchi and wrapped them into a cloth bundle. She dropped the bundle into a plastic bag.

"Take this with you when you leave," she said.

"Thanks halmeoni."

Daniel had the line hooked to the bamboo pole.

"We don't have bait," LJ said.

"We can dig up worms by the creek."

At the creek, LJ and Daniel threw the line out in the shadiest part of the water. Daniel went for a swim while LJ made small piles of rocks around the dry part of the creek.

"Hey, did you bring any of that beer here?" Daniel asked.

"Yep."

"Nice."

"Hey, you're gonna get sunburned. You and your white flesh."

Daniel returned to shore. LJ handed him a beer.

"The tide is going to come in in a bit," he said. "We should build something."

"OK. What should we build?"

"I don't know."

Daniel squatted down and picked several rocks about the size of his palms. LJ watched.

"They should be flat stones. Let's pick the flat ones. Do like Goldsworthy did," LJ said.

Daniel tossed aside the rounder stones and collected the flat stones—dark blue and dark brown, some covered in green algae.

Daniel began to build a circle, piling the stones on top of one another to gain the right balance. LJ wandered further away from the pile of stones and brought them for Daniel to use. The circle's diameter was about thirty inches, and the height was equal to its diameter.

"This needs something else," he said.

Daniel dug a hole in the same diameter beside the structure they'd built. As he dug, the water from the creek filled the hole.

"We could put the fish we catch into this waterhole," LJ said.

"We could."

"We could but… that might kill all of them."

"The tide's going to come back in eventually."

"So this well we built is going to go under?"

"Yep."

"How long do you think it'll stay in tact?"

"I don't know. Maybe a month?" Daniel said.

"A month?"

"I think so. There might be some trace of it for a while but yeah, I'd give it a month."

"That's so depressing," she said.

Daniel reached into LJ's bag and handed her the lomo camera. She snapped a few photos of the structure, the waterhole, the creek, their shoes on the stones, the trees that hung over the creek water, downward from the slope of the hill, and the mountain that loomed before them, covered with the yellow fuzz of the chestnut trees.

"Grab your shoes," Daniel said. "We should catch the bus back."

43

Stupid Jobs

"How long were you in Korea?" Meeja asks me.

"I was there since last July."

"And you just got back?"

"Yes."

Arnold comes up to Meeja saying, "Ahjoomah," then yawns in her face. He makes a noise like a dinosaur.

"What? What you want?" Meeja says. Arnold laughs then elbows her in the gut. Meeja pushes him away. Arnold looks at me and cracks up. I wink at him. Jose grins as he watches the two of them from the other end by the grill.

"What were you doing in Korea?" Meeja asks.

"Not much. Drinking a lot. Meeting a whole lot of people. I did some research. Some reading and writing."

"Were you going to school?"

"No. Translating literature."

"So were you getting another degree?"

"Um. No. Just doing it on my own. They gave me this grant to do it. Paid me to live there for a year. It was a low-pressure situation."

"What are you going to do now?"

"This," I say, pointing at the floor.

"Don't you want a job?"

"I was at an interview yesterday but I'm not gonna take it."

Meeja clicks her tongue.

"What?" I ask.

"That's stupid."

"Maybe. Maybe working there is stupid. Working here and at my other job is pretty stupid, too."

"Rotten girl."

44

Deaf Arnold

Two Indian men wearing glasses walk up to the deli glass and look at Arnold.

"Do you have wedge-a-tarian sandwiches?" the shorter one asks.

"Hah?" Arnold says, turning his head to side, leaning in.

"Wedge-a-tarian."

"I can give you a sandwich with vegetables on it. You want that?"

"How much would that be?"

"Eight ninety-five."

The shorter Indian man turns to the taller Indian man and says something.

"Okay, we'll have two plain bagels. One toasted with butter, the other untoasted with cream cheese."

"Comin' right up." Arnold fixes up their bagels and hands them to me. I put them into a brown paper bag and hand it to the shorter Indian man.

"Two seventy," I say. The shorter Indian man opens up one of the wrapped bagels and looks inside.

"This is not what I ordered," he tells me.

"What is it?"

"I asked for a toasted butter bagel and an untoasted cream cheese bagel. That guy had it wrong."

"Arnold," I say.

"What?"

"That guy's complaining."

"What?" Arnold says to the shorter Indian man.

"You gave us the incorrect order. We asked for a toasted butter bagel and an untoasted cream cheese bagel."

Arnold makes an invisible gun with his finger, raises it to his own head and pulls the trigger. He dangles his head for a moment with his eyes closed. Meeja and I watch. The shorter Indian man stands still and stares at Arnold silently.

Arnold takes the two bagels from me and tosses them behind the deli counter. He pulls out two more plain bagels and cuts them in half. The shorter Indian man continues to glare at Arnold.

"I'm sorry," I say to the shorter Indian man. "He's hard of hearing."

The shorter Indian man's face softens a bit.

"Oh, is he really?"

"Yeah. I apologize," I say.

"No, no. It's fine."

Arnold is deaf in his left ear. On average, he gets about three orders wrong per day because he doesn't catch what a customer is saying. Meeja once told me that a customer stood there, watching Arnold pile cream cheese onto a bagel and shouting at Arnold to stop, but Arnold kept slathering it on because he couldn't hear him. Another time, a customer asked for French toast but Arnold gave him an order of French fries instead. The customer was so angry that he shouted at Meeja, asking her why the hell a deaf guy was working here if he couldn't take people's orders properly.

The Indian men leave. I ask Arnold how his hearing went wrong.

"I got hit by a truck," he says.

"Stop shitting me."

"Three times," he says and raises three fingers. "Same side." Arnold turns his head so show me the left side of his face. His ear looks fine.

"But why's it always the ear?" I ask.

"You keep gettin' hit by trucks and it eventually takes a toll on your hearing, na mean? I mean it hits my body but after three times…"

I laugh.

"The second time it happened, I went to the same hospital up in Queens. And the doctor was like, 'You *again*?'"

"No, I still don't believe you, Arnold."

"Well, believe what you want, baby."

45

Filipinas

A herd of middle-aged Filipinas enters—six of them. They chatter loudly.

"Oh my god," I say. One of them, a short one with glasses, short bangs and a black dress approaches me.

"We come here yesterday. We meet maybe twenty people here," she says.

"Oh my god," I say. I look around for Meeja.

"Ahjoomah!" I shout. Meeja walks up to the front of the store. She sees the group of women and says, "Hi. How are you?"

"We come here yesterday."

"I remember," says Meeja. "Okay. Come to this register. I take care for you."

Meeja and the short Filipina chat. The rest of them hover around the deli, looking and pointing at things, talking to one another. One of them brings over a pack of gummy bears and shows it to two other women and says something. The three of them start to laugh.

One by one, the women begin to bring containers of foods and wax paper wrapped sandwiches to the register with their choice of drink. I jot down each item they bring onto a long piece of memo sheet and hand it to Meeja.

"Okay. I'll take care of this. If they say they're part of the group and bring any more stuff up to you, just send them to me," she says.

Meeja's good at handling large orders. I usually find them too overwhelming. Not too long ago, a man from Madison Square Garden came over one afternoon, requesting a large order.

"I'm gonna need sandwiches to feed about fifty big guys," he said to me. I called for Meeja and she took care of everything. The entire deli glass was cleaned out—all the sandwiches and paninis were gone. She cut the guy a good deal, and threw in a few bags of chips along with the order. The man said that he'd be back.

The Filipinas continue to talk very loudly, but most of them are really funny. One of them picks up a banana from the basket and says, "Excuse me! How much for bba-na-na?"

"Fifty cents."

"Oh! I take four."

She and her friend stand by the basket and look for the spottiest four bananas they can find. She hands me two bills and walks upstairs to join her party.

Arnold takes off his apron and steps down from the platform. He heads towards the bathroom with a T-shirt in his hand.

"It's time for me to go," he says.

"Gonna go get a few beers now?"

"Yeah. But I have to go visit my son first. After I go visit him, I'm going home to get my beers, smoke a joint, take a nap, then go to work in Brooklyn by five AM. Workin' seven days. Just like you, except you too young."

Arnold returns to the front in his change of clothes—a

black t-shirt and a Nike backpack. He looks different without the plastic apron and paper hat.

"See you next week, hon."

"Bye, Arnold."

46

Toro y Baca

"Oye, Jose," I say. "Is pastrami beef?"

"Sí."

"So what's the difference between that and roast beef?"

"No se... Um... Maybe pastrami es toro y pastrami es baca."
Jose laughs hysterically. I don't say anything.

"Comprende?" he asks.

"No."

"One is toro, the other one baca. Both beef." He laughs
hysterically again.

"Yeah, that's pretty funny," I tell him.

A Russian man enters, wearing the Thirty-fourth Street
Partnership uniform and hat. He's the one who replaces the
garbage bags for the trash receptacle right outside of the store.
He has a black mustache that looks closer to blue and a very
pale, wrinkly face. He is short and has a potbelly. He always
comes in for two bananas.

He walks straight up to the banana basket repeating softly
to himself, "Banana, okay, big one," over and over. He takes his
hat off and examines them one by one.

"Oh my god..." he says, picking up the fruit.

"Yeah, I know. No good today," I say to him.

The Russian garbage man prefers the unripe bananas. If
there is a single brown spot on the fruit, it is immediately

rejected. He also always makes sure to get the largest two bananas from the entire basket.

"No. No good," he says. I reach for the very bottom of the basket and find one banana without any spots on it. When I show it to him he says, "No. Not big enough. I want the bigger one," waving me and my ridiculous banana away.

"Sorry."

"Ah," he puts on his hat, turns around and leaves.

I look at Jose.

"The guy just wants the biggest banana," I say. Jose laughs hysterically again.

I pull out a few cigarette carton memo slips and walk over to Jose. I write down a bunch of random numbers.

"How do you say this?" I ask.

"Noventa y seis."

"What about this?"

"Setenta y siete."

"This?"

"Quarenta nueve."

"And this?"

"Cinquenta."

"You're a good teacher, Jose. You should teach Spanish." Jose smiles.

"Thank you. I need to know cause some of the customers don't understand what I'm saying, you know?" I say.

"Yeah. You learn. It's good for you. Your Spanish is good."

"Gracias."

"De nada, mi amor."

I look at the register and see an old Latina woman place

two Styrofoam containers onto the scale. The total comes to twenty dollars and thirteen cents. I tap on the register screen.

The older woman hands the girl five singles. The girl takes the singles and shoves them back into her mother's purse.

"¡Ay caramba!" the mother cries then whacks the girl on the shoulder. The girl pulls a credit card from her wallet and hands it to me.

47

An Emergency

Meeja and I put Orange Tree Delicatessen stickers onto the yogurt parfaits from behind the deli counter. A large Chinese woman walks up to the counter frowning.

"Excuse me!" she screams, her face contorted in pain.

"May I please use your bathroom? It's an *emergency*!" The words squeeze out of her like air escaping a rubber balloon. I grab the bathroom key tied to a long block of wood and hand it to the woman.

"Oh my god. Thank you!" she says, taking the key from my hand. She rushes to the back of the deli. I look at Meeja and laugh hysterically.

"If you waited just one more second, she would've shat her pants," Meeja says in Korean.

Twenty minutes later, the Chinese woman returns to the front of the store with sweat beaded around her forehead.

"Thank you!" she says and places the key on top of the deli glass. Meeja doesn't look up. I look at the woman and laugh. The woman chuckles as she walks out.

48

Thieves

Jose walks up beside me.

"They drink a soda," he says, pointing at two tall teenagers, one black and one white. The black kid is wearing black-framed glasses, jeans, a blue sleeveless top. The white kid has a red hat and a green backpack.

"What do you mean?" I say.

Jose walks off the platform and goes over to Pedro. Pedro hands Jose two green aluminum bottles of Sprite. Jose brings it to the register. I shake them. Empty.

"Who drank it?" I ask.

"The boys over there," Jose says, pointing at the two teenagers who were bringing a plastic container full of mac and cheese, fried chicken, lo mein noodles, and potatoes. They place it on the scale. They weigh over three pounds.

"Twenty-four forty-nine," I say to them.

"What? Oh, hell no," the white kid says. "Let's get out of here." He walks out of the store first. The black kid with glasses follows him.

"Ay," I say. The boy stops. "Pay for these sodas right here."

"We didn't drink it," he says.

"Why are my guys telling me that you did?"

"I paid that guy," he says, pointing at Pedro. I look at Pedro. He shakes his head.

"I thought you said you didn't drink it," I say.

"Alright, how much is it," the boy says, reaching for his wallet.

"Two dollars each. That makes it four."

"And how much is this food right here?"

"Like I said, twenty-four forty-nine. So you owe me twenty-six forty-nine."

"Alright, hold on a minute," the boy says. He walks outside and joins the white kid. The two start to walk down the street.

"Uh-uh. Jose, get them." I say. Jose runs out of the store with Pedro following behind him. A minute later, Jose returns with one kid and Pedro the other. Both Pedro and Jose each have their hands wrapped around the kids' wrists. I've never seen either Jose or Pedro look so angry before. Jose is biting his lower lip, and his forehead is smooth.

"Yo, let go of me," the black kid says. He struggles from Jose's grip. Jose's a lot shorter than the boy. The white kid struggles to break free and Pedro loses his grip, but grabs the kid's backpack then holds him back. Jose and the other kid begin to stumble back and forth. A thirty-something-year-old white man wearing headphones and checkered shorts walks in, looks up, then stumbles back out of the store.

"Just pay for the fucking soda!" I say.

"I didn't drink it!" the kid yells.

"Want me to roll the cameras?" I say.

"Go ahead! Roll 'em!"

"Fine. I'll call the cops. And we'll roll it while they're watching."

I go to the phone and dial 9-1-1, muttering.

"Punk ass motherfuckers, stealing sodas, not paying for their fucking food…"

"Yes, hi. This is Orange Tree Deli. We're on Seventh Avenue between Thirty-third and Thirty-fourth. A couple of kids here won't pay for their items."

"Alright, we'll send someone right over."

I place the phone back on the receiver.

"Just sit tight, and we'll let the cops deal with it," I say.

"Alright, fine. Fine. I'll pay for it. Jesus," he says.

"No, no. You don't need to. Just sit tight. We'll let five oh handle this."

Meeja takes four dollars from the boy.

"Just let them go," she says to Jose. Jose releases his grip. The boy looks at Jose then walks towards the door, shaking his head. Pedro lets go of the other kid's backpack and he follows suit.

"I better not catch you motherfuckers back in this store again. Get the fuck out of here," I say. The boys leave. Jose returns to his post behind the deli glass and leans against the grill.

"Jose," I say. "I've never seen you like that!"

Jose laughs.

Two white cops—a woman and a man—enter the deli with a hand over their guns.

"Someone made a call?" the woman asks.

"Yes. But they left. Forget it," Meeja says.

"Okay." The cops leave.

49

Row House

The phone rang.

"What are you doing?"

"I'm sleeping. Oh my god," LJ said.

"Well, stop sleeping. Come outside. I'm outside," Daniel said.

"Okay."

LJ got out of bed. She looked at the time on her phone. Four a.m.

"Oh my god," she said. She went into the bathroom, tied her hair back and grabbed a blue sweater off the chair by her desk.

LJ pushed out the door of her building and saw Daniel standing in a gray hooded sweatshirt, shorts and running sneakers. He grinned at her. When she drew close, he patted her head.

"Why the hell are you at my apartment at four in the morning?"

"I couldn't sleep. So I went for a run. And then I ran to your place."

"Oh my god."

"Stop saying that. Let's run together."

"No. I am not running. I just woke up. Let's go inside. We'll sit inside."

"I don't want to sit inside," Daniel said, pacing. "Let's walk somewhere."

It was dark out save for the orange light coming off the street lamps. The night was very quiet but they both listened for sounds while walking silently.

Up ahead, they both saw a small hill made of pavement. It had a steel fence that ran along the side of it with flowers and shrubs behind it.

"It can get depressing sometimes," LJ said.

"What can?"

"Walking the same path over and over again. The same walks. It can get very depressing."

"Yeah. It can."

"Is that why you called me?"

"What do you mean?"

"It's nicer now, isn't it? In the night? When it's quiet?" LJ asked.

Daniel didn't say anything. He reached for LJ's hand. They walked until they arrived at a massive staircase. Sounds of the highway could be heard. LJ looked down as she ascended the stairs with Daniel.

At the top of the stairs was a long walkway, which led towards a bridge. It was like two halves of a circle were placed together with the curved backs touching, creating an apex. In between the frame of the two halves were giant steel bars in a crisscross pattern, creating a truss over their heads as they walked beneath it.

"What a magnificent bridge," LJ said.

"Seriously. It's beautiful. Look at this massive arch."

"This is such a tiny bridge in comparison to the bridges

they have in New York but I like the quaint style. What bridge is this anyway?"

"I don't know. We'll find out later."

"I can't tell what color it is. What color is this?" LJ asked.

"Red."

"Really? How do you know?"

"I've seen it before. I went on runs down this path before," said Daniel.

"Oh."

They both fell silent again. Below them was the Han River. Up ahead were giant buildings with lights.

"I can't tell if this is scary or beautiful," said LJ.

"Stop talking so much."

Cars rushed past them. They walked on silently until they reached the other side of the river at Yeouido. They walked down a paved walking path with a large slope that fell down to the right of them. At the bottom of the slope was another walkway, then some stairs. Down the stairs was the Han River Park, which led pedestrians all the way to the water.

LJ and Daniel walked through a large dark tunnel of trees.

"This is a little spooky," said LJ.

"How is it spooky? I'm right next to you."

"This is really spooky. What if someone finds us and murders us?"

"Want to see what's *actually* spooky?"

Daniel led LJ by the hand towards the base of the bridge nearer towards the river. Giant concrete columns supporting the bridge loomed ahead. LJ looked at the grassy area to the left of her and saw a few people scattered, lying down on broken cardboard boxes.

"This water here is full of dead people," Daniel said.

"Ew. How do you know?"

"I just know. I know because a bunch of people jumped off the bridge to commit suicide."

"Jesus fucking Christ. Why are we under a bridge, Daniel? This is where homeless people hang."

"Look up," Daniel said.

LJ looked. There were steel catwalk structures over her head.

"Wow."

"I want to get up there."

"No. You can't. It's locked."

"It's not locked."

"I'll bet you a million dollars that it's locked," said LJ. "We shouldn't be here."

Daniel put his hand down LJ's back then nudged her closer to him.

"You're gonna let some locked doors stop you?" he asked.

"Shut up."

LJ let go of Daniel's hand then walked up ahead. Daniel followed from several feet behind. She looked at the park. The lights were bright orange and glowing. The sky was growing a little bit lighter. She continued to walk with the river running to the left of her and green buses moving on the far right up ahead. She saw a convenience kiosk up ahead and ran into it.

The fluorescent bulbs were overpowering. She went to the fridge and grabbed two cans of Hite beers and brought them to the register. She handed the cashier a bill and the cashier returned her change and the beers inside a black plastic bag.

Outside, Daniel stood with his hands in his pockets looking at LJ.

"Where are you taking me?"

"There's a row house I found near here. I'm taking you there."

"Fine." LJ handed Daniel a beer. She cracked hers open.

50

A Smile

"Something's wrong," Meeja says. She walks over to my side of the register from the other end of the deli.

"Why?"

Meeja reaches for the bathroom key.

"Whenever I eat, I have to shit," she says.

"Well, that's normal. That's good."

"Not when you go every single time you eat something." Meeja walks to the back of the deli and into the bathroom.

A fat white man in his fifties wearing gray cotton sweatpants, a blue tracksuit jacket tied around his waist, and a stained white wife beater carries a Styrofoam container to the register. Strings of mozzarella, brown sauce, and tomato sauce cover the sides of the container. The man's red face is covered in sweat and grease. He has warts on his nose, enormous purple lips, yellow teeth, and giant blue eyes. He wears black headphones attached to a CD player that sticks out of his fanny-pack.

"Hey, you," he says to me.

"Hi." I weigh the container.

"Twenty-three nineteen," I say.

"Hm… You know what, I'm just gonna fill this up to an even twenty-five, how's that for ya?" The man removes the container from the scale. He walks back to the buffet. The steel plate on the scale has streaks of grease and sauce. I pull Windex out from under the counter and spray the scale. I grab a few napkins from the cardboard box beside the register and wipe down the plate. The fat white man returns to the register. He plops the container back onto the scale. The price screen reads, "25.69." I look up at the fat white man. He is shoving a piece of fried chicken into his mouth.

"Sir, I'm gonna have to charge you for that," I say.

The fat white man stops chewing and looks at me blankly.

"Well. I'm kidding, but next time, please don't grab food from the bar with your hands without paying for them."

The fat man resumes chewing without taking his eyes off of me. I punch the numbers into the register and hit the tax button. The man hands me a twenty and a ten. I returned his change.

"It's to stay, right?" I say.

"Yes. And I'd like a smile," he says. I throw plastic utensils, napkins and the container onto the tray and look up at him.

"And I'd like a smile," he repeats. I feel like throwing up. My forehead tightens. Meeja returns to her side of the register.

"Next!" she says.

"Ahjoomah, are you feeling okay?" I ask in Korean, ignoring the fat white man who continues to stand there, waiting for a smile.

"Yeah."

The man picks up his tray with his grubby hands and carries it to the back of the deli. A large sweat stain covers his back.

I shiver as I look on. I look up and see Meeja counting

dollar bills and tying rubber bands around bundles of fifty-dollar bills.

51

Clocking Out

Around a quarter to six, Mr. Kim strolls in. He waves at me before going to the other register counter and grabbing a red T-shirt. He goes into the restroom to change. When he returns, he tells me, "Go eat."

I grab a paper plate, a handful of napkins and go to the salad bar. I pile kale leaves and radishes on my plate. At the hot foods area, I grab a chicken leg and a pile of mac and cheese.

Pedro walks behind me.

"Comida," he says.

I turn to him and grin.

I take a seat in the back. I notice the white lady who comes in and buys a soda and bagel everyday. She uses the deli bathroom to apply makeup. Usually by the time she leaves the deli, dragging her belongings shoved into a beat-up black luggage on wheels behind her, her eyes are caked in black eyeliner. She's sitting about three feet away from me, counting change on the green tabletop. She's wearing dirtied-white fingerless gloves. Her fingernails are painted black. Blonde hair juts out from underneath her black baseball cap. Her knees are sunburned, exposed from her torn jeans. This woman is generally very happy whenever I see her. She's also extremely polite at the register whenever she buys anything.

She finishes counting her change, places her hand on the handle of her pushcart and looks out at the deli.

Next to me is the black tour bus ticket guy. He's in his red hat and vest. He always buys a cup of coffee and two bananas during the day. He comes in several times throughout my shift to use the restroom. No questions asked. Our eyes meet. He smiles a little bit and nods his head. I salute him with two fingers to my forehead.

After I finish eating, I look at my phone. A text message from Mary: "LJ! Are you still coming to my reading tonight? Afterwards we're going to a bar on Manhattan Ave.

They give you a ticket for free pizza if you buy a beer. Come get it!"

I toss my plate, say goodnight to Mr. Kim and leave.

52

Sidewalk

Outside the deli I see Oskar pouring bleach and water from two plastic jugs onto the sidewalk next to his ice cream truck.

"What are you doing Oskar?"

"I am cleaning the sidewalk because those guys won't do it."

Oskar points at the retail store in front of us.

"You're a good man, Oskar. Good, clean man."

"Yes. It is so filthy. I can't understand why they would want to keep it this way. I don't want my customers to stand here where it's dirty. They should think of their customers the same way."

"These guys are retail, buddy. They don't need to care about their customers like that."

"Are you leaving now, LJ?"

"Yep. Heading to Brooklyn to see friends."

"Well let me give you a sample."

"No, no. I'm okay."

"No, please. You will advertise for me."

Oskar goes into his truck.

"Cone?"

"Yes."

"Vanilla or chocolate or combination?"

"Black and white, Oskar."

Oskar pulls down the lever and fills the cone with a swirly soft serve.

"Thanks, buddy."

"You're welcome. Have a great time. See you tomorrow."

"Okay, Oskar. Have a good one."

53

Harassment

On the six train, I think about how many flights of stairs I have to climb later. The thought of it kills me. I feel miserable. My legs and feet are so swollen that I can feel a throbbing in my shoes.

I get out at Fifty-ninth Street, take the escalators up and walk north on Lexington. A thirty-something year old Latino man in a dark green shirt, jeans and a cigarette looks at me as I walk by him in the opposite direction, passing a deli. I hear him make smacking noises with his mouth.

"Hey miss. Why you frowning, today? Smile, girl! Smile!"

I can feel the pressure on my forehead as my eyebrows crumple. An angry heat rises from my gut and reaches my throat, turning into a stone right below my tongue. I stop breathing for a second. I continue to walk then resume my breathing. I cross the street towards the east side of Lexington and Sixtieth Street.

Every time a man harasses me in the street with catcalls or a comment about my look or telling me what I should do with my face, I get angry. Whether what the man says is harsh, lewd, or a simple greeting is a non-issue; none of it is better or worse than the other. They are all equally terrible and infuriating. Why people continue to think it's okay to tell me what to do, or suddenly try to speak to me on the street, or make kissy noises in my direction is beyond me. I will never understand it, and I refuse to accept it. The only thing I can possibly do about it is hope that it will completely stop.

Back at the apartment, I take a shower under cold water and massage my feet while crouching down on the tub. I get out, dry off then blow dry my hair. After reapplying some makeup, I change into a backless blue dress, ankle boots, then step back out.

54

Brooklyn

I reach the bookstore on Manhattan Ave forty-five minutes later. The reading is held in the basement. A guy sells PBR cans for three dollars. I take one, drop the bills and crack it open. I see Mary's boyfriend Sam, and her cousin Gina. I wave. They gesture to come sit by them.

"How are you guys?" I hug Gina and Sam.

"Thanks for coming, LJ," Sam says.

"Of course."

The reading lasts one hour with five performances. A girl sings a song accompanied by her guitar. It is improvised. She sings about how she's from Virginia. Other than that, the song is completely pointless. A guy goes up and tells a story about his pet ferret. A woman goes up with a man and they do a small performance about a newly married couple. The fighting seems very real and intense. People feel uncomfortable. When it's over, people seem relieved and they clap. Mary reads a prose poem from her latest publication. It starts out on endive salad then ends on something related to the apartheid. Her reading is the final performance. People applaud.

The group moves to a bar next door. Three of Mary's friends are there. Mary introduces them to me. Alice is a black-and-white film photographer, who works a day-job as a receptionist at a realtor's office. She lives with her boyfriend Bruno, who is a graphic designer for a popular blog that publishes articles written by twenty-something year-olds. He is also a video artist. Gary is a telemarketer. He is also a writer trying to get a book of essays published.

"This reminds me of a line in *Serpico*," I say.

"What line?" Mary asks.

"How all of your friends are on their way to becoming somebody else."

Bruno laughs.

"It's true," he says.

"What's *Serpico*?" Gary asks.

"I'm not insulting you guys. I'm in the same boat. I was a deli girl today for twelve hours. I'm pretty exhausted," I say. Alice nods her head.

"Go get a beer," Mary tells me. "They give you a ticket for a free pizza."

I order a Blue Point at the bar. The bartender gives me a ticket. One of the performers from the evening is standing next to me. It's the guy who played the male counterpart in the newly wed performance.

"Hi," I say.

"Hello."

"Do you want my ticket?" I ask.

"Sure. Thanks."

"Where's your wife?"

"Oh—that's my roommate."

"You're an actor?"

"Yes."

His name is Charles. Charles buys me a drink in exchange for the pizza ticket.

"What do you do?" Charles asks.

"I write."

"Cool. Where at?"

"On my computer."

"I see," he says. He takes a sip of his beer.

"I do a bit of copyediting during the week. And I work a register on the weekends," I say.

"Isn't there an easier way?" he asks.

"Is there one for you?"

"No. I guess not. Well, I work on weekends, too, but I have off at least a day during the week."

"Rest is important. Even God rests," I say.

"What do you write?"

"Prose. Essays."

"Can I see them anywhere?"

"Yeah, on that website that Bruno maintains," I say.

"Who's Bruno?"

"Mary's friend."

"Oh, I see. So you know Mary through writing."

"Yep."

"Ah. Where you from?"

"Here."

"Your family's from New York?"

"My parents are from Korea but I grew up in New York."

"I see."

I invite Charles to our table. Gary, Bruno and Alice recognize him.

"You were good," Alice says. Gary looks at Alice who is smiling at Charles.

"Thank you."

"Yeah. You're funny. You're a funny guy," Bruno says.

Bruno resumes his travel story, which we'd interrupted.

"I was driving through Uruguay with friends. And suddenly a huge rock smashed straight into our windshield. There was glass everywhere. My head was cut open and bleeding. My friend wasn't hurt but pretty freaked out. So anyway we stopped the car and got out to see what the fuck was up. And these guys with knives appeared. They took our wallets then drove away in our car."

"Oh my god. What did you guys do?" Alice asks.

"We just walked. The house we were trying to get to wasn't too far. But yeah. It was pretty freaky."

"I'm not sure if I believe you," Gary says.

Bruno shrugs then sips his beer.

"Where you from, LJ?" Gary asks.

55

Brooklyn Bridge

Charles calls a cab. We board it together. Charles asks me if I am Chinese. I am turned off by the question.

"No. I'm Korean. Are you Dominican?"

"Yeah. How'd you know?"

"I guessed. You said your family's from Washington Heights."

The cab moves swiftly past two cars that have stopped and pulled over to the side of the road. I only catch a glimpse of the two men standing outside of their vehicles looking at each other. One of the cars had hit the other car from behind.

"Have you ever seen people have an argument over art?"

Charles thinks about my question for a moment. He turns to me and nods his head.

"Yeah. I see it all the time actually. But I think they fight because they're not supposed to be working together in the first place."

"I mean, if you were to give it a word, the thing that they fight over, what would you say it was?"

"I'm not sure. Just a difference in their definition of art maybe..."

I nod my head and look out the window. The lights pass. The freeway is winding. I'm not sure where we are. There's an overpass above us. A minute later we're on the Brooklyn Bridge headed into Manhattan.

"This is a magnificent bridge," Charles says, looking out the window. I nod my head.

"Yeah. Sometimes when I'm feeling kinda blue, I take the Q train in from Manhattan into Brooklyn just to see it from a distance."

Charles nods his head.

"Yeah, I think I get that."

The cab pulls up at my building. Charles and I hand the driver a wad of bills then we get off.

"I have to be up at five tomorrow morning to be at work..." I say.

"Why? Where do you work?"

"In Midtown. I work from seven to seven."

"Okay. That's fine."

By the time we reach my door, Charles and I are out of breath. I tell Charles to be quiet as we pass Annie's room. After we both enter, I close the door shut.

56

Row House II

The row house looked more like an abandoned shack. It was painted blue on the outside and had a flat rooftop. The entrance was on the side—a giant white door without a lock. Daniel pushed it to the side and it opened roughly, sliding left. The inside housed several rowing boats and oars placed upright against the walls. Towards the back were a couple of rowing machines. There were two windows on each side of the house. One window had broken glass and a tree branch grew clear through it. On the cement floor right below it were scattered brown leaves and pieces of glass.

LJ pointed at the broken window, looking at Daniel.

"That's the sort of thing I mean. I think houses and buildings should all have one of those," Daniel said.

"But it's a hazard."

Daniel grabbed a few square cushions from a shelf. They were foam cushions covered in blue synthetic. He dropped eight of them on the floor then looked at LJ.

"I feel like a chick in some movie about depressed suburban kids who have sex on mattresses next to abandoned cars," LJ said.

Daniel walked around the small bed he'd created. He grabbed LJ's hand and pulled her down towards the floor. As the sun rose, an orange light covered everything outside. It grew brighter as the minutes passed. Soon, there were people jogging, walking and riding bikes along the river.

57

Seogang Bridge

I go to the bathroom and shower. When I return, Charles is sleeping on my bed. I sit beside him wrapped in a towel.

"Hey," I say.

"Hey. Hi," he says, touching my leg.

"Would you mind leaving?"

Charles lifts his head from the pillow.

"What?"

"I have to get up early tomorrow and I can't really sleep with you here."

"Oh. Oh—okay. I understand."

"Sorry. And thanks."

Charles gets dressed. I remove the towel and put on an oversized T-shirt.

"Bye," he whispers.

"Bye."

I crawl into the sheets and listen to the door close behind him as Charles leaves. My head is loud with the sounds from the day. There are a million voices erupting at once and I can't decipher whose is whose but they all sound familiar. I can feel myself clinging onto something, like I don't want to fall.

I am at a house, standing on the second floor with low hanging ceilings that make it feel almost like an attic. I run my hand over a large tabletop made of wood but still not properly sanded. The splinters grate my fingertips as I walk towards the window. My bare foot touches the dark wood floor—smooth, thick, and warm like smooth stones below a moving river, rounded out from time, taking in the heat of the sun. As I walk across it in slow steps, I listen to it creak below my feet. I get closer to the massive windows, and my hand reaches for the lever to push it open. I can identify the sounds before I even look out the window: massive trees with the wind rushing through them, and birds chirping inside, unseen from the thick of the green, and the sound of water moving over and through the rocks on a creek.

I reach the window then immediately shut my eyes. The images appear in the darkness behind my eyes: four streams of water making vast streaks across the page; big strokes that cut across the material and divide them into five sections; the Hudson River running on the north west, the East River down the south east, the Han River cutting straight down the middle between the two bodies, and the Cheongyecheon creek running quietly at the very southern section. The landscape is speckled with millions of small squares; inside each square resides a small circle, which appear like mandalas and together form a vast cityscape, fused densely together by an infinite range of ideas; the Han River trickles down and floods around the edge of the concrete land block to meet the start and the end of the East River; the mandalas arranged to illustrate curves that ripple out from edge of each river, assembled in patterns to create a larger circle, divided by the river's section to become semicircles, save for the very top piece, where the starting point of its land is the edge from an unknown larger body of water and the other edge met by the Hudson River; a giant circle forms from the middle, spreading out in all directions with its small compartments, each one uniquely drawn, meditated to form at the instant of its creation, and the next compartment drawn completely new, and different from the previous formation; each line scrawled anew to four edges that become a square, and then another line that starts from a dot, goes around and meets that same dot to form the broken edges of the circle it created, giving each compartment's residence its own single character. The forms continue and spread.

The alarm goes off. By the time I get ready and step out the door, it is six. I walk past the fruit cart. The guy looks up at me and nods his head. I nod back and walk south then westbound.

PART TWO

"Man is made in such a way that he continually has to define himself and continually escape his own definitions. Reality is not about to let itself be completely enclosed in form. Form for its part does not agree with the essence of life. Yet all thought that tries to define the inadequacy of form becomes form in its turn and thus only confirms our tendency towards form."

–Witold Gombrowicz

58

Race and Class

I have no idea what I want to do or what I want to be. I only know that I want to evolve.

It is important to question one's own integrity and principles. It is important to do this daily. This is why I think it is important to think, write and forget. Move forward. Let the mind evolve. Nothing else matters.

Curiosity is a good state to begin anything in. Not rejecting an idea entirely also sits alright with me. Who can know or choose an absolute completely? (How crazy of an idea is that, and what would the point of living be if one is suddenly entirely sure of herself?)

I have no religion, no country, no ideology, no culture, no ethnicity, no race, no name, no gender, no identity—I am nothing.

Bukowski says that ones who start wars are usually the ones who preach peace. Urban professionals that I've run into these last few years, the same ones who claim political correctness, culture and intelligence turn out to be the most annoying people, the same ones who'll bring any news item in the *New York Times* about Korea to my attention. Why? Why does anything Korean-related have to be some reason to notify me? People around me who only see me as one way are the ones who do this. Their sole interest in talking to me is to remind me that I am Korean. I have worked for people who do this, I have met them in schools among both peers and teachers, I have close friends who do this, I have friends who claim to be scholars and anti-racists who do this, I run into strangers in the street, restaurants, cafes, subways, buses, airports—all over the world—who do this. And these kinds of people are always the same ones who preach against racial discrimination.

How can one claim to be a racist, really? On that same note, how can one claim to blindly love one's own country so confidently? People are surprising individuals. Each person is so full of unknowable things, and those things are themselves constantly moving and changing. The collection of individuals that are spread across a piece of land that is then called, "Country" is not a singular wholeness but a multitude of ever-changing, unplanned, unforeseen circumstances and possibilities. It is just as ridiculous to claim hatred against an entire group of people just as it is to claim love for an entire group of people. Without knowing each and every individual exactly for who they are (which is constantly changing!) how can one really do this?

Newspapers are only there to tell people that there are reasons for tragedies but really, there is no concrete reason for violent acts. Newspapers are phony. News sources are phony. Nothing should ever be written with such authority and spread around so vastly through the channels that exist today. It hurts everyone because it is loud and arresting, and ultimately distorts the actual instance of the moment it is trying to reiterate.

Derrida said that in Algeria, where he was born, "all sorts of racisms were at work in all directions." He said that everyone could at the same time claim to be a victim of racism while participating *in* racism. This was true for Jews, Italians, Algerians, French-natives—basically anyone who resided in Algeria. Derrida's point is that everybody is a victim of racism and is a racist at the same time, but one will never claim to be a racist because we believe ourselves to have reached a point in astuteness today.

When I was six, my father told me a story. He said that during Korea's colonial days, if an insurgent was ever captured by a Japanese officer, a way to torture him would be to hang him upside down by his feet. Then the Japanese officers would boil water, add red pepper flakes then pour the mixture down the insurgent's nostrils until his belly got full. Then an officer would cut the rope so that he would fall to the ground, at which point the Japanese officers would collectively stomp on his belly with their boots until it burst.

"They were really messed up, those Japs," my father said. "They did a whole series of things like that. And they did horrible things to our women, too. Awful people, those Japs."

When I was twelve, on our drive home after a bizarre after-school health seminar about puberty, my mother said, "The Japanese used to put our women in tents then send in their soldiers to rape them, one at a time. They did this because their own women were full of venereal diseases from prostitution. But think of what the soldiers were carrying when they came to gang rape our women."

At a certain point in my life, I realized that I did not want to carry on my parents' politicized strife, which stemmed from years of nationalistic education and anti-foreigner (anti-anyone-non-Korean) propaganda over the years of rebuilding the country after the Korean War. Neither of their families had any money, and they grew up without very much to eat. I'm sure they've been told that their hunger had something to do with foreign invasion. Both have a very clear understanding of what starvation is like. My mother once told me that as kids, she and her sisters threw saccharine over prematurely plucked tomatoes to mask the unripe flavor. They did it because there just wasn't anything else to eat. Whether or not these memories are blown out of proportion is really not my own to call. If my parents have memories like this, they have them because that certain past has etched something inside of them. They may at times romanticize the memories or turn them into moral-driven fables for me to appreciate what I have now, but these memories are not my own. If they are, they are by proxy. My own objective is irrelevant to their pains, and I had to consciously overcome the biases that they raised me on.

My every effort during college was to see and know what my family considered "taboo," so I began to take an interest in Japanese literature and films. Sometime after that, the natural thing for me to do was shift back to a nationalistic stance and pursue Korean literature, with the blown up vision of being the greatest literary translator there ever was, while shamefully wondering why it was that I hadn't done it sooner. But after having done so thanks to the residency period I had in Korea, and having seen that field and academia for what they are, I now know that I don't really need to do much of anything. There's plenty of work being done and plenty work that is not being done. Regardless, I'm not interested in that route. All these firm points, charged discussions, papers and books exhaust me to no end, and they turn literature into personal agendas masked by politicized reasoning. I have zero interest in it. I care nothing for it. I'd rather continue my cashier work and eat unripe tomatoes covered in saccharine.

I was and still am attracted to the Korean intellectuals of the modern era who were unable to come to an agreement on a single idea in order to liberate Korea from Japan. And these men, in their state of frustration and longing to uphold the ideology that seemed so clear in each of their own minds. As a whole, they produced a diverse body of work. Following them, in the post-Korean War modern era, a number of women began to publish books with a tremendously imaginative and bold voice. They dominate Korea's literary world today.

In 2009, I saw a film called *The Viewfinder* by Kim Jeong. In it, a Korean animator says that he was laid off at work because a Japanese man came to take his place; the character says that the difference between a Japanese man and a Korean man is that a Korean man's imagination knows a limit, which the Japanese man does not know. The reason, he says, is because a Korean man's consciousness is aware of a certain kind of pain which he experiences during his military training. The pain contains an awareness of a reality he never should have known, and it anchors him to the earth, stifling his creativity and the mind's ability to reach the heights of imagination.

What the character left out in this monologue is that the women of Korea are not forced into such a heinous obligation. They are untouched by militaristic awareness and the pain that comes from training. They are free to see, think, imagine and create as they please, and the women certainly do as writers, poets and filmmakers. So after all these years, it's now the men who are facing the blank canvas and page, muttering to themselves, "Men can't paint, men can't write." It is up to the women but not just any women, but the conscious women—women who know how to trust and challenge themselves.

I wish to evolve. I'm learning how to trust and challenge myself, and I will arrive.

59

The Middleman Minority

Korean immigrants began to operate green groceries in black neighborhoods in the 1970s. The middleman minority theory hints that wherever the majority (white) doesn't want to operate their business in a minority's (black's) territory, the middleman minority (Asians) uses it as an opportunity to run their own business. Examples include trends from the 1960s, when whites did not open stores in black neighborhoods, so Chinese immigrants opened stores in those neighborhoods instead. Then Korean immigrants began to flock into the US in greater numbers in the 70s and 80s. Koreans were accused of taking over black businesses and taking money away from local neighborhoods.

From 1981 through 1995 there were a total of fifteen boycotts organized by blacks against Korean owned businesses. The longest one lasted seventeen months, at a couple of grocery stores in Flatbush, Brooklyn. During the LA riots in 1992, the violence reached a point of firebombs, shootouts, and breaking and entering. The newspapers always quote the most racist remarks that Koreans make against blacks and that blacks make against Koreans.

Some folks around me today still have quite an angry reaction to the memory of that time. It was rough but things like that happen frequently and not just here in the US. In the end, it's not about blacks versus Koreans. It's about what the media says about relationships between groups of people of color, differentiated by the majority's perspective. What is said in the media should never be taken seriously. Images and scenarios get blown up to the point of being false, and the moment is abandoned by becoming mediated by a different party with its own agenda—the majority's agenda, the agenda of those in power, the ones who don't wish to share it or give it up.

The mainstream view of race is taught by those who claim a belief in political correctness, and claim to provide an objective viewpoint during "competitions" between two or more groups that are, supposedly, busy hating each other. This lie is perpetuated constantly in our newspapers, textbooks, television screens, etc. The mainstream observer continues to fuel that fire with the majority's mediated stories. The groups in standoff will read it, and their anger will rise. The distrust will continue. Race is a mediated concept. It was mediated by the person in charge, and for the privileged person whose needs are sustained by differentiating groups according to race.

A properly fleshed-out story, a proper history, a real look is never illustrated by those who handle the media you consume, so discard your televisions, ignore your newspapers, and ignore your parents, teachers and presidents.

Stupid crimes that make no sense and have no real reason or logic behind them happen everyday. In the emotional chaos that begins with marginalization then instigated by a white cop murdering a person of color and getting away with it because this country and its laws are still crooked and oppressive, the majority mediates, beginning with sound bites, footages and photos taken out of context and displayed as the truth—hateful "truths" that will continue to blind people of color with anger and turn them against one another. Disasters like the LA Riots happen all over the world, but are exasperated by the mainstream media and its lies. People don't understand that the conflict between groups—groups differentiated by the majority by color—is triggered by the same people who utilize newspapers, teachers and presidents to keep oppression and anger in a continuum. Why it takes us forever to understand this is another business I'd like to discuss but perhaps in a different book with less bitterness between my teeth and less pain inside my chest.

People who've worked too hard and seen too little from it are naturally frustrated. When the fuse gets lit by something like a hate crime, it doesn't take just one person to create destruction to the point of costing nearly a billion dollars. If the mass is a collection of hurt and distraught individuals, if the mass is a collection of folks who share the same grief and pains of marginalization and inequality, if empathy runs on all levels here and there, across persons, then the impact of what's to come from that anger can be great.

What causes us to one day find ourselves standing in the middle of a battlefield with planes flying over our heads, bombs blowing up in the distance, and bullets speckling the bodies and earth all around? Whose agenda is it that we are a part of? While standing in silence, listening to the commotion, we'll ask ourselves the same question and hope for a response. Please remember that many people in the history of our human kind have asked this question (or are currently asking this question) then died without ever hearing the answer.

There is a responsibility in you, and in me, to get to the bottom of things, down to the core of the comfortable fluff we are surrounded by and face the prickly realities that make our bloods boil, visions turn red with anger, and our minds nearly collapse in exhaustion from being overwhelmed. That reality is difficult because we have been pacified and injected with ideas of political correctness, and to consider discussions on race taboo. The anxiety and discomfort which have been injected into us over the years with the Majority's lies centered on race and political correctness need to be exorcised, detoxed. Then dismantle the structural biases that exist in you and me that have been handed down from the Majority's anxiety over losing dominion. It'll take a lifetime but you and I will get there.

I have but one goal in life: it is to evolve.

60

Groups

In her essay "On Truth and Reality," Anais Nin paraphrases her therapist Dr. Otto Rank: "...group activities weaken our will. They may be a solace to our loneliness, but they do not foster the individual creative will." I've always had a problem with groups on a cultural level, religious level, national level and nuclear level.

Groups must collapse. Any establishment must always be on the verge of collapse the instant it realizes that the texture around it is starting to grow firm with development. When people suddenly come together to develop an agenda based on an idea, it becomes a militia. Groups must collapse and disperse and become new and separate groups. And those groups must never exist for too long; as soon as a group comes to a general consensus or agreement, it must disappear and become another thing immediately. That is the group I'd like to be in—the kind that would accept me as its own then immediately disappear no matter how "good," or "humane," or "moral," or "necessary" or "safe" it claims to be. No agenda on earth should ever be seized with importance. Think of how small and quick and fragile life tends to be. So why invest in what is said to be the "importance" of things? The earth and all its contents are too diverse for anything to ever impose itself onto a different thing. And all life is is but a constant rallying back and forth between one thing or another. Decisions tend to be made arbitrarily. It's better not to invest in any sort of beliefs. They'll only wear you out, and leave you with nothing.

Why do people say that humans are not meant to be alone? That's crazy to me. Aloneness is the sake of being human. In my greatest state of solipsism I am aware of two things: a tremendous pool of shame, the size of Lake Erie inside of me, and another lake right beside it feeding me with the heroic feeling of being Human. At this point of inner conflict there is the greatest amount of possibility. This is progress, and just one person should be at the work of her own progress. If we all admit to our co-existence of shame and greatness to just ourselves, as an individual—just me to me, and you to you—there may be hope for a greater progress just yet. To quote Nin further: "It is necessary to establish this first before engaging in group activities. For Dr. Rank, the supreme achievement was this creative will which could resist brain washing of various kinds...We should not bring to the collective an unfinished, distressed, chaotic, confused, sick or hurt self."

Let's work on that. I am working on it. I have a plan; it is to evolve.

61

Family

I am never at ease with family. Having grown up as an only child with just my own two parents around, I never had a definition of family. None of my cousins lived near me, nor did my aunts, uncles and grandparents. They were all in Korea and I was always here in New York, and I moved out to live independently as soon as I turned eighteen. The concept of 'family' is foreign to me.

When I returned to Korea for my residency, I visited my relatives for the first time in almost twenty years. Eating and sitting in a circle of adults while little kids ran around the room, I realized how little tolerance I had for the whole experience. My relatives, who said that it was important that I eat there with them because I was, after all, family, overwhelmed me with pressure. I wanted nothing more than to leave and be alone somewhere with a pack of cigarettes.

Being told that I was the only one who had gone to school and grown up in the US, my relatives all looked at me with a certain expression, which was a mix of envy and awe, a look of wanting me to take them with me when I returned to the States, or call upon them once I made it big in the land of opportunity. I hated this look. And I realized how the word "family" was just a word—a tool—to oblige people with responsibilities. The word had no meaning or value to me because I never understood it in my upbringing. I decided not to feel so guilty after all. I owed these people nothing and they didn't owe me anything either. The pleasure of meeting someone who knew me because my parents knew them was something I did not share. Whatever expectation they had of me solely due to the fact that a blood relation was at work was a non-issue to me. Until the day my maternal instinct kicks in to have a child of my own, I will never associate myself with the belief that one must be willing to die for a family member solely because he or she is a family member. That, to me, is just as ludicrous and irrational as saying that a man or woman must be willing to kill or die for the sake of his or her country or for his or her religion. I have no interest in that sort of fundamentalism.

62

A Korean-American Alien

In both the US and Korea, I am an alien form. I am not accepted as a whole or complete person anywhere. Wherever I turn, I have to explain myself with a few extra words, providing a little bit more background information—always. This is the case no matter what.

Derrida says there are clear distinctions among things that come "close to the proximity" of racism and those that are actually racist. When people pose what they believe to be a harmless question, it feels like an obligation to answer it, and that obligation is an incredible imposition. The question demands some sort of explanation of myself, and who but criminals and delinquents in our history are required to explain themselves? My physical self having the general appearance as Asian demands an explanation of me always, and I feel obliged to answer them, but that doesn't lessen the imposition by any means. I hate this extra task I am assigned just by the way I look.

I am not offended. I'd need to be able to defend myself in the first place should it be an offensive thing. But it's not that. The questions I am asked which arise from my appearance come from a place of curiosity and concern (but why even take it on as a concern in the first place?).

When I'm manning the register at the deli or on the elevator with a delivery guy or in a meeting with someone for the first time in a general social setting or at a job interview, I get asked questions or I am offered unsolicited observations about me being Asian or Korean which come close to the proximity of being racist but are not quite so, and yet still, when I am put in that position, I get mad as hell. Because it's an imposition, you see? Not an imposition in the definitive sense but more in the basic sense, in the sense that you who ask this question are imposing onto me a form, and not only that but you are forcing me to answer to that form, become it, describe that form to you, explain it and give that form words that might sound the most familiar to you, in which you might have the capacity to associate with, with whatever words you have in the corpus of your mind. What a savage act.

At times like this, I feel twice as angry as I might if someone just straight up called me a "chink bitch" or "gook cunt," because that would at the very least contain a refreshing sense of straight-forwardness as an insult rather than be delivered with layered confusions, multitudes of conflicts and explanations tied to the insensitivity that You initiate by posing what seems like an innocent question or remark in the open realm of our society. You will always have a constant outlet by pleading ignorance to it all, especially when You begin to panic at my visceral, negative reaction, then make *me* look like the crazy one with the problem. Fuck You.

Perhaps the mistake is in one making the assumption that I may hold all the answers to all things Asian and/or Korean-related; the pressure is enormous, and think about it: How would you feel if you're suddenly put on the spot to speak on behalf of all Asians, Koreans and Korean-Americans? Isn't that silly? All you can do when a person makes a general question regarding all Asians to you is to simply speak for yourself from your own personal experiences and knowledge as best you could. But they must be careful not to see you as just that—simply a lens into all of Asia—either. But they won't bother with their own shortcomings at this juncture; you're the one in the hot seat. So answer yourself!

The pursuit of an entire continent and all its containing countries and neighboring countries, the history of each, the culture from each, the customs of each, the people and the individual existences of each and the infinite makeup of each—this is a tremendous task, and shouldn't it be obvious? Perhaps the imposition exists only because I create it. I can't say that I am not to blame, either. I *must* be blamed. The question that is asked can be as simple as, "Does your countrymen not shake hands? Do they bow instead?" can be answered with a 'yes' or 'no,' should I be the kind of person to not give a shit; if I wasn't aware of modernity, Westernization and the transition, and the layering and the push and pull, the conflict and confusion of Korean history that I associate with that simple question, I would be able to answer with a 'yes' or a 'no.' But I can't, and people simply aren't interested in hearing somebody out for that long, so I won't.

Maybe that person was just trying to start a conversation... but maybe I just cannot allow myself to be reductive in any circumstance no matter what because it is wrong, offensive and the sort of thing that the mainstream media teaches.

Ever since "The East is a career" was declared, world wars have taken place, airplanes invented, books written, movies produced, and the internet invented for an infinite amount of information sharing to occur. Should one have a genuine curiosity and concern for what is Asian and/or Korea-related, one may go to the relevant sources to satiate such curiosity. There are other ways to find out about a country and its customs, culture, history and all of its contents. There are other ways to get to the bottom of things without interrogating me about it, who just so happens to be a Korean-American woman.

These "close to the proximity" of racist remarks are hardly even understandable to me mentally. I just know how I feel when I hear them: a slight shock, a rising heat to my face, a tightening in my back, neck and shoulders, a discomfort in my stomach, a coldness in my hands and feet. If I have such a real and physical reaction to something, shouldn't that be enough of an indication to know that it is wrong?

I don't have an intellectualized answer for you on why it is wrong. People talk a lot, though. A lot of money is spent on education to get these answers, and I am in a great deal of debt because of it, but this question never seems to get answered. Or maybe you just don't have the time for it. Maybe you just don't care. Then why do you continue to pretend by asking shallow, meaningless and offensive questions?

Wars happen around the world because of something as stupid as ideology. So do brawls and fights in the streets and in schools all around the world, everywhere—all because of ideology. Another ideology is not the answer to a visceral problem. The mind will never fully intellectualize what the body feels sometimes. If I just understand my anger at another person's imposition against me as 'heat,' I can live with that. College, religion and politics never made sense of these issues for me anyway. The problem lies in the belief that there is an answer to something so complex and unintelligible. The answer is definitely not political correctness, which winds up alienating more people in the long run and mystifying identity even more. My body is not a political or philosophical object. And I consciously refuse to involve my mind in the aforementioned entities. No *one thing* will ever resolve it for me once and for all. This is a part of the process—part of the evolution—and I am on top of it.

The hope is in the point of flattening the planes, and destroying what completes itself as Form, which then designates its own significance onto itself *and* imposes it onto others. Making, creating, establishing and abandoning is an act of progress—the kind I can live with until I arrive.

Bad questions are asked daily. I wish to evolve and get away from these bad questions.

63

A Schizophrenic Child

I've only heard of this in a movie once. Apparently there is a highway that can connect Asia with all of Europe. One can start at the lowest tip of the Korean peninsula, say Busan, then reach the far Western hemisphere in Germany or France, if they wished, just with a car, or the other way around. Imagine the range of experiences and possibilities a person would be opened up to if this were to happen.

A person, instead of flying over the continents and its numerous countries, missing out on all the action below, would instead drive through the countries and take in a range of experiences, opening up to people in the places they travel through, taste the food, learn things, exchange dialogue and perhaps find a new sense of him or herself through the travels, and gain a deeper understanding of the people of this earth—the billions of them. Imagine this being achieved by just a highway.

What gets in the way of South Koreans to embark on this journey is North Korea. Entry is not allowed, at least not without extreme control and regulation, and exit out through the Chinese border is, of course, completely outlawed. The problem about this restriction on zones and boundaries is more universal. If we really think about it, one must question the necessity of boundaries, zones, and areas where land gets cut off and designated as a place for certain people, etc. Just look at how many families are kept apart for generation after generation because of ideological differences.

And it's funny to me how overfed countries constantly participate in the global problems. They offer charity while also holding those same countries at gunpoint and producing weapons of mass destruction while warning others not to do it. They plant military bases all over the world, especially in smaller countries, or countries that were won over in wars decades ago. Then they go around loudly preaching about freedom, peace and god. To think about it all day is enough to make the blood boil—enough to make one feel completely hopeless about absolutely everything.

The scholars of today who've studied those figures and others are helpless idiots. They have nothing but words and theories. They have nothing but useless knowledge and offer no solution. Buying knowledge is expensive in this country. But it ends there—simply working as a commodity and bringing no peace anywhere. Just more anger and frustration.

Translation of modern Korean literature was not at all a rational decision, rather one that occurred from a great deal of noninterest. In college I studied comparative literature, and while doing that, I took up some writing classes in memoir, poetry and fiction. I took to one writing professor especially—Gerard, a historical novelist. He's the one who asked me if I wanted to translate any Korean fiction into English, and I wasn't sure why he was asking me this. He then asked me if I was fluent in Korean, and I wasn't sure how to answer this either. I knew Korean because it was the first language I was ever exposed to at birth, and I had learned to read and write it at nursery school in Korea as well as at home from my parents, and the multitude of Korean children's books we had in the house. But I never gave translation the slightest thought until he asked me that question.

Given my grasp of both English and Korean on an intuitive level, translation of words or interchanging them in my head was natural to me—not even a conscious thing to be made of. It was just something I did my whole life. Knuckling down and actually applying this to task was something I had to learn how to do. I practiced by translating poems from Korean into English. The poems I chose were primarily the ones written during the Japanese occupation of Korea in the 1900s, which I did mostly out of curiosity. Having grown up in a household filled with anti-Japanese sentiment, I wanted to read what the voices of those who lived through that period were like.

At the end of the fall semester of my senior year, Gerard emailed me an application for a grant to translate literary works abroad. I wrote the proposal indicating my interest in modern short fiction written and published during the occupation because of the diversity in their voices. Although they were all Korean by nationality, each author's work sounded very different from one another. It was difficult to lump them into categories. Some of them resembled the French, others Russian, still others German. Some of them sounded more sentimental and idealistic; others were gloomy but glossed with a sense of humor. These writers were layered by multiple identities, cultures, ideologies and consciousness; they were all born in Korea and educated in lands elsewhere, such as China, Russia and Japan; they were not allowed to travel to the US due to friction between Japan and the US;

European and English literature entered their minds via Japanese translated texts. The layering and mixture, the conflict and the enlightenment, the weight and confusion are endlessly embedded in them and apparent through their works as a whole. This is what I learned while translating the short fiction works in Korea over a span of one year. I translated twelve short stories, all written and published in the colonial period, and wrote a paper on modern intellectual Korea's struggle to attain oneness as a nation during that period of explosive dialogue for what each intellectual thought was right for his or her country. The pressure eventually broke the nation into two.

Korean intellectuals, quite a few of them driven by frustration of their unemployment and frustration with inapplicable ideologies swirling inside their heads, wanted to overthrow the Japanese and failed to do so. What is in part to blame is their intellectual ego, which they'd thrown at one another amongst themselves as a group at the discussion table, and existing day by day as unemployed, aimless, penniless and stifled men who pronounced a right to deserve greatness and comfort, because that is what education had promised them, at least in the examples they saw among the Japanese and Europeans. In order to forget this disappointment, visits to the red light district were frequent. Getting drunk was on the regular.

The hilarious thing about the modernists' agenda is that they wanted a unified Korea before it even split up and became two. The idea was to unify Korea under a single ideology, come together as a single force and overthrow the imperial regime. The smart and vocal ones wrote out whatever Western idea he picked from his studies in Russia, China or Japan on a large picket sign and raised it high. From a birds-eye-view, the sides seemed split into two primary colors—pro-socialist versus pro-capitalist, but variations of both were prevalent and among the polarized groups were factions, too. The battle of egos among Korean intellectuals, the lack of jobs in a saturated job market among educated men who were in competition with one another and with plans to put their minds into use in revitalizing their nation, the frustration of not seeing their hopes become a reality, and the continued shadow of oppression from a foreign government kept them busy, angry and confused. Intermittently political activity to boycott or overthrow the imperial government bubbled up, but was quickly extinguished by imperial forces. During the years that drew closer to WWII, Korea was regarded by Japan as another Japan. After Japan lost the war, Korean intellectuals were still engaged in a battle of deciding which concept was better—capitalist or socialist. The fighting led to a civil war. Eventually, Russian and US forces stepped in like divorced parents ready to leave the house and go off opposite directions; they split the child in half in its most vulnerable and uncertain state. To this day the child struggles with identity issues. It sees itself as two separated parts—as two halves—not a whole, and the rest of the world regards it as so. A schizophrenic country, helpless on its own and with the thumbs of outside forces stuck in its mouth to keep it pacified, silent—to prevent it from crying.

64

"A Society That Drives You to Drink"

There's a story written by a Korean modernist who studied in Shanghai. He published a short work of fiction called "A Society That Drives You to Drink" in 1921 in a small socialist magazine, which is narrated in the third person but seen from an uneducated woman's point-of-view. She wonders why her husband, in spite of returning from his college education abroad in Japan, continues to sit at home doing nothing, complaining of his frustration and going out to get drunk all the time.

The intellectual husband in this story comes home one night, incredibly drunk, and complaining about his society and the learned men who meet at discussion houses to have stimulating conversations about the different kinds of ideologies that they've each learned about during their studies abroad. And the men have a heated discussion about whose word trumps whose at the table. The story illustrates a sad depiction of minds that have gained a great deal of knowledge and insight but physically, in their occupied country, the men are not able to get jobs and unable to agree on a single mission to pursue together as a group to bring the nation forward independently. The husband in this story addresses his wife while really just asking himself and to no one at all a very important question: what is it that makes a man cripple a great and competent mind with drink? The question is rhetorical, and the answer does not lie in the title of the story either. It is not the society that drives him to drink—that would be too much of a cop-out. It is himself. His own frustration at his inability to gain any satisfaction from his day-to-day, and the reason why he makes his mind dizzy with drink is because his body is so still, so trapped and stifled there in the room next to his idiot wife, who doesn't even understand the word "society," when he says it, because she has no concept of it.

The husband is frustrated at many things at once and at himself: he is angry at the Korean economy for not being able to provide jobs to learned and capable men like himself; he is angry that his country has not educated women that he must marry and live with, who are unable to holdup, what seems to him, like a simple conversation; he is angry at the lack of proper infrastructure and leadership among the intellectual community to oppose and overthrow the Japanese imperial government that has been occupying his country for over a decade now; he is angry at his own impatience and his own incompetence, and therefore he drinks till he is crippled and forgetful, deeming his knowledge useless. I see the same amount of frustration among my peers. They feel the same way whether they are employed or unemployed. They don't believe that books have taught them anything useful. Just ideology that will forever leave them frustrated with their current system. But in that frustration and lack of resources and capital, how are we to make change? How are we to make an ideal a reality?

I've stopped wondering. Why must we try to change people's minds? We as individuals are only capable of changing ourselves. It is good to think. It is helpful to write. I don't believe in anything else. My whole life, someone else has been trying to change my mind or impose a certain image or a label on me. Am I a woman? Am I Asian? Am I American? Am I Korean? Am I Korean-American? Am I a working-class person? Am I an intellectual? Am I of the one point five generation? Am I a Christian? Am I an atheist? Am I a Buddhist? Am I a Buddhist by proxy? Am I a republican? Am I a socialist? Am I a democrat? All of these are the wrong questions to ask me and yet I am asked these questions everyday, ordered to define myself for others to do as they please with the information. Who am I? I am nothing if you ask me these things. I don't wish to matter to anyone to whom these questions would matter.

Identity is transient and fickle—constantly changing. It is never an absolute. A person is only a person because she pursues the act of becoming a person everyday. When Yi Kwang-su writes in *Mu-jeong* that an individual must always strive to become a Person, he wasn't being existential knowingly; he'd unwittingly touched upon a revolutionary and popular idea at his time: one can never simply be but must always become, constantly, until death.

If one is already at a state of absolute, one is no different from being dead. How utterly boring it must be to claim being in such a state... how can anyone be so sure of who she is when immediately after she establishes herself as something specific in her mind, she is already no longer that and has already moved on to becoming the next thing?

(Do you know me? Must you know me? Stick around and see if you find what you're looking for or for as long as you need to. Whether you choose to stay or leave is irrelevant to me and more relevant to you and your mission. And even if you leave, I'll be an image inside your head unchanged, but outside of it, I'll be moving forward on my way to becoming and becoming and becoming. I have but one goal in life: it is to evolve.)

PART THREE

"We might have the most brilliant, the most feasible ideas for the amelioration of this or that, but there is no vehicle to hitch them to. And what is more strange is that the absence of any relationship between ideas and living causes us no anguish, no discomfort. We have become so adjusted that, if tomorrow we were ordered to walk on our hands, we would do so without the slightest protest. Provided, of course, that the paper came out as usual. And that we touched our pay regularly. Otherwise nothing matters. Nothing. We have become Orientalized."

–Henry Miller, *Tropic of Cancer*

65

Sunday, August 22, 2010

Walking towards the deli, I see a truck double parked next to a green van with a sign that says 'Bartlett NY' on it. A black man with a green shirt, gray gloves, khaki shorts and black boots unloads a crate of milk, helped down by his partner. The sight elates me. It feels good to be up and about so early in the morning. Mr. Kim looks up at me while bagging two wax paper wrapped sandwiches as I stroll in.

I bow and say 'hello' in Korean.

"Good. You're here," he says.

I go to the register on the opposite his. I pull the hair ties off my wrist and tie my hair into two pigtails, letting them trail down my chest. Pedro carries a stack of orange trays and places them on the counter. He nods his head at me.

"Buenos dias," I say.

"Buenos dias."

I look ahead and see Armando by the grill. I wave at him. He grins and waves back.

"How are you, Armando?"

"Bien. You?"

"I am *really* tired," I say.

I look at the door and see Mr. Moy strolling in.

"Ay! Good morning, LJ," he says.

"Hey, Mr. Moy!"

"French toast for you today?"

"Okay."

"Alright. Six pieces for you."

Mr. Kim pats Mr. Moy on the shoulder.

"Busy last night?" Mr. Moy asks.

"So busy. Go crazy," Mr. Kim says. "So much fighting."

Mr. Moy goes to the grill and scrapes the surface. He squats down and grabs a bag of Texas toast from the shelf below the deli glass and pulls out three pieces of bread.

"Okay, LJ. It's all yours," Mr. Kim says in Korean.

"Any fights last night, Mr. Kim?" I ask.

"Yeah. I wish I could curse and scream like you, LJ," Mr. Kim says.

"No, it's really unpleasant."

"No, really. I'm jealous. And I wish my daughter could speak Korean as well as you."

"My Korean's okay. Not great."

"No. My daughter's twelve and she can't string together a single sentence properly without mixing in English. It's a problem."

"That's not a problem, Mr. Kim. Your daughter's alright."

Mr. Kim grabs a plastic bag from the shelf behind me and walks to the back of the deli, into the bathroom. He returns wearing a different shirt.

"Okay, Moy," he says. Mr. Moy looks up from the grill and waves.

"See you later tonight," Mr. Kim says.

"Bye, ahjuhsshi."

"Oka-y-y-y, LJ. For you," says Mr. Moy. He places a

Styrofoam plate with six pieces of buttered French toast next to me.

"O-o-o-oh."

"I know. This piece biggest one. Ha ha!" Mr. Moy says, pointing to the biggest piece.

"Thanks, Mr. Moy. Looks amazing."

I go to the fridge, grab a carton of Eden's organic soymilk, shake it, and pour it into a cup. I fill the cup with coffee from the dispenser then insert a dollar into the register. The color outside the glass doors looks lighter than just a few minutes ago.

There's a green van parked in front of the deli that I've never seen before. Inside, I see a large Latina woman wearing a lot of makeup and a gray hat. She is sleeping. There's a younger woman on the passenger's seat sleeping, too.

I see Oskar's ice cream truck pull up beside the van then slowly move forward. The truck stops, and I see it double park beside another van.

Pedro pushes a large sign with a list of breakfast specials and their prices out onto the sidewalk. People pour in. The grill and deli counter gets busy with orders. People order two eggs on a roll, French toast, pancakes with sausages, sides of bacon or turkey bacon, ham and cheese on croissants, bagels with cream cheese, wheat toast with butter, et cetera. It gets busy.

A few minutes later I hear arguing. It's Oskar's voice and another man's voice. I glance outside but cannot see either of them. I only see the large Latina woman with the heavily made up face and the younger woman unfolding a table and putting out wool knit hats, Pashmina scarves and sunglasses out on display. I can see the older woman looking at the men fighting.

66

Rooftop Party

Maria and Antonio were throwing the rooftop party at a space reserved for them in Gangnam, sponsored by Absolut vodka to promote a library project in Istanbul. There were caterers grilling steaks and bartenders inside a large plastic water storage tank lit up with green and red lights, serving cocktails.

"Hey, can you do something for me?" LJ asked.

"Sure."

"Will you design a house for me?"

"Okay. What kind of house do you want?" he asked.

"I don't know. Just make it an interpretation of me through you."

"Okay. Yeah, I can do that."

They were sitting on outdoor furniture—large white mattress-sofas, and looked like little square islands.

"I have something for you," LJ said, reaching in to her purse. She handed Daniel a densely rolled up piece of paper tied by a blue string.

"What's this?" he asked.

"I translated a few poems by Yi Sang and typed it out onto this long receipt roll that some ahjoomah gave me at the drug store. She said she had no use for it so I took it."

Daniel removed the blue string and the paper unraveled loosely. He looked over at the words.

"Interesting," he said.

"I figured why not make use out of an old and discarded thing like that. I thought you might appreciate it. Since Yi Sang was an architect, I figured you might find something in his language that speaks to you."

"Thanks. I love it." Neither spoke for a few minutes as Daniel continued to read the written content.

"This is inward-outward process," he said. "It's a step closer to the substance before form. I really like it," he said.

Daniel looked at his phone then excused himself. LJ went to the bar and got a vodka on the rocks. When she returned, someone had already taken her seat. LJ saw Daniel walking back onto the rooftop with a woman. LJ looked at her without saying anything. Daniel introduced the woman to LJ.

"This is Mona. Mona, this is LJ."

Mona sat down beside LJ. Daniel excused himself to get Mona a drink. LJ asked Mona how she knew Daniel. She explained that she was a graduate student and in the same program as Daniel. LJ nodded.

Daniel returned with two drinks in his hand and gave one to Mona then leaned back against the mattress sofa and began to chat softly with her in Korean. LJ turned her head and looked out at the crowd. She noticed a sharply dressed white man and a tall Korean woman standing beside another white man with long hair. She recognized the sharply dressed man as the Italian fashion designer she'd met at a different party a couple months ago. She also recognized the wife. The wife had complained to LJ about how much she hated the way Korean men ate soup:

"They're so loud! They slurp and they're messy. Then they

pick up their bowls and drink it down in gulps before slamming them down on the table. I don't get it. Korea needs to fix so many manners."

"Where's the bathroom?" Mona asked.

"Downstairs."

"I'll be back," she said. Daniel watched Mona walk away.

LJ looked at Daniel without speaking. Then they both heard arguing. They looked up and saw a short Korean guy wearing glasses arguing with a very skinny girl wearing a fedora and a black and white striped shirt. The girl was taller than the guy. She was leaning very closely into the guy's face. The guy's face was slightly turned to the side, as if to avoid eye contact. The girl kept saying to him,

"What? What? You have something to say to me?" Their friends stood behind, trying to pull each of them aside.

Daniel turned to LJ:

"They're engaged, those two."

Mona returned. She smiled nervously and she sat back down beside Daniel. He leaned his head back again and began to say something to her quietly with an affectionate look.

A girl from the party approached Daniel. LJ recognized her from Daniel's studio. She'd screamed at him about the screwdriver. She took his hand again and led him to the opposite end of the floor. She sat him down beside some older men with beards and glasses. He shook their hands. The girl spoke in Korean and the men with beards and glasses nodded.

Mona turned to LJ and asked her what she did.

"Um. I'm a writer," LJ said.

"Oh. What do you write?"

"Um. Stories, I guess. Stories. And I translate other people's stories."

"Oh. So are you a translator or a writer?" Mona asked.

"Um. I guess I'm both."

"What do you translate?"

"Modern Korean literature."

"Oh. I see."

LJ and Mona fell silent.

"Do you have a boyfriend?" Mona asked.

"No."

"Oh. Is there anyone you're seeing?" she asked.

"No."

"Is there anyone who likes you?" she asked.

LJ let out a snort.

"How would I know that?"

Mona let a moment pass then said,

"Do you like anyone?"

LJ didn't say anything for a few seconds then said,

"No. Why do you keep asking? Do *you* like someone?"

"I like Daniel," she said flatly.

LJ excused herself and went over to Daniel.

"I'm leaving," she said.

"Hold on," he said. "I'll come with you."

Daniel went over to Mona and said something. The three of them left the party together. They walked towards the main road where LJ noticed the girl in the fedora who had been fighting with her fiancé trying to hail a cab. LJ asked the girl if she was okay. A cab stopped in front of them. The girl in the fedora let out a huff and said that she was really pissed. She told LJ to take the cab then walked away.

LJ turned and saw Daniel and Mona standing behind her, talking. LJ opened the cab door and went in first.

"C'mon, let's go!" she said.

Daniel asked Mona if she wanted to come with him. Mona said that she was headed in the opposite direction.

"Well. You can come over if you want," Daniel said.

Mona shook her head. Daniel reached out and hugged her briefly then got into the cab. The car moved onto the street then onto a highway.

"You're an idiot," LJ said to him.

"Why am I an idiot?"

"You should've let her take this one and sent her off first."

"Really? Should I get out and do that?"

"Well, it's too late now. We're moving."

"Oh. Do you think that was bad?"

"Yeah. It was pretty bad," LJ said. She turned her head and looked out of her side of the window. The lights flashed by quickly. They gave LJ a headache. She closed her eyes.

"Is that the girl you're seeing?" LJ asked.

"Oh. Yeah. Did you figure that out?"

"No. I didn't. She fucking told me," LJ said.

"Yeah."

"Hm. Who is she?"

"She works at the Hyundai department store, but she takes a few art classes at my university. I like her drawings but she's too passive when people critique them. I'm trying to get her out of her shell."

"What do you mean?"

"I mean she should be more outspoken about her intentions

and what she wants. She lets people make changes to her style constantly to the point where there's nothing left of herself."

"Well, that's her problem. Not yours. Stop trying to change and fix everyone."

"But that's what I feel like I'm put here to do. Like, someone to liberate them…"

"You're being really condescending to Koreans right now. You should stop thinking this way. And if you want to keep thinking this way, just go back to the States."

"Well, I'm not though. I'm learning plenty from the people and teachers here. But at the same time, I feel like I could teach them something about being fearless in art and making big strokes, and pushing bolder ideas…."

"Shut up. She's boring. I don't like her," LJ said.

"She has three huskies."

"So many shallow girls love big dogs. They pretend like their lives have meaning by raising enormous pets that require a lot of care and attention. My ex recently married one of those," LJ said.

"My ex-girlfriend left me six months ago but I know she still loves me."

"You're in denial."

"We're broken up and we've recently stopped speaking to each other but I know that she still loves me and I love her."

"You're a bastard."

"Why?"

"For bringing me here," said LJ.

"I don't understand," said Daniel.

"You're so selfish and needy. I don't need to see other girls you want to see and I don't need to hear about your ex girlfriends. You always need some girl to be around for you to fuck or call and have over when you're feeling bored and lonely. It's so damn shitty of you."

"Don't say that."

The cab moved below an overpass. To the left was the Han River, glimmering with orange light. The cab filled with silence. They both listened to the tires hum across the highway's pavement.

"Hey, check out those lanterns," Daniel said. "I said look. Look at those lanterns! Ah, fuck. You didn't look... You missed the lanterns."

"I saw the fucking lanterns."

"No, you missed them."

The cab pulled up at a street in Hong-dae. Daniel reached out and hugged LJ then got out. The cab pulled back onto the street and headed north. "Pretty Maids All in a Row" began to play on the radio.

"I like this song," LJ said to the cabbie in Korean.

"Oh! You speak Korean?"

"Yes."

"I love the Eagles. I used to listen to them all the time when I first started driving cabs. Do you like Elvis?"

"Um. Sure."

"Gee. I love Elvis," said the cabbie, shaking his head in delight.

LJ watched restaurant signs flicker brightly as the car moved past them.

"Miss, can you tell me something?"

"What?"

"Why do Korean girls like American men?"

"You mean why do Korean girls like white men?"

"Yeah. American men."

"I don't know."

"Really?"

"I guess because they can speak English. And that way Korean girls can learn to speak English." LJ said.

"Ah. I see. Are you Korean or American, miss?"

"I'm both."

"Ah… I see."

67

Butter Roll

"¿Habla español?" a woman asks. She's short with light skin and bobbed, brown hair. Her husband has a mustache and a blue-checkered button down shirt.

"Un poquito?" the husband asks. I nod.

"Ah. Muy bien. Por favor, un pan…" the woman says, making a circle with her hands, "con mantequilla." The woman butters an invisible piece of bread with her hand.

I begin walking towards Mr. Moy.

"Tostado?" I ask her.

"Por favor," the woman says, widening her eyes.

"Toasted butter roll, please," I say to Mr. Moy.

The woman and her husband walk to the coffee counter, rapidly speaking in Spanish, and fill two small cups with coffee. The woman turns to me.

"Y leche?" she asks. I point at the gray compartment with three dispensers.

"Ah," she says. The woman returns to the register and says, "Suca?"

I point at the sugar jars on the coffee counter.

"Ah!" the woman cries. She returns to the coffee counter, picks up the sugar and pours it into her cup. Her husband stands by her and watches.

"Gracias," the husband says when he and his wife return

to the register. Mr. Moy hands me a Styrofoam plate with a toasted butter roll, cut in half.

"Como se llama un pan con mantequilla?" the woman asks me.

"Butter roll," I say.

"Buh-ler-loll," the woman replies.

"Butt-er roll," I say.

"Butter-loll," the woman says, wrinkling her eyes and nose. She throws her hands into the air and says,

"Muy difícil."

The husband begins to say something rapidly in Spanish. All I catch is "Barcelona." The woman laughs.

I tap on the register screen.

"Five sixteen," I say. The husband pulls out his wallet, hands me a five-dollar bill then opens his palm revealing a fistful of change. I find a dime, a nickel and penny and say,

"Good." I give a small wave.

The husband picks up a quarter from his handful of change.

"Cuando?" he asks.

"Vente cinco."

He picks up a dime.

"Cuñado?" he asks.

"Diez."

"Y esto?" he asks, raising a nickel.

"Cinco."

"Y esto uno?" he asks, holding a penny.

"Yes."

"Ah. Ok. Gracias."

I nod at them. I hear the woman say "buh-ler roll" again as she walks to the seating area. The husband picks up the orange tray with the roll, croissant, and two coffees, says, "Gracias" to me, walking towards the back to join his wife.

68

Parking

Oskar brings a small pouch folded out of a napkin.

"Good morning, Oskar."

"Here. From my house to your house," he says.

"Thanks. Chocolates?"

"Yes. It is American, but tasty. A new product. With peanuts."

"I noticed a new vendor," I say.

"Yes, the woman from Mexico. She's selling hats and scarves. It's still warm out, though..." Oskar looks around the deli with his hands at his sides. He has crow's feet around his blue eyes. They droop down a bit on the sides, and he always looks sad and innocent like a newborn animal.

"Hey, what happened earlier? Have a little spat?"

Oskar shakes his head.

"That man is a grand maniac. He sells handbags on the South West corner," says Oskar.

"Was it over a parking spot?"

"He has ten feet of space right in front of him, but instead of moving up, he tells me to move back. The guy walks around the street," Oskar puffs out his chest and pulls his arms back to imitate,

"like he owns the place. Everybody has a problem with him.

That skinny girl there," Oskar points at the skinny Mexican girl selling hats, scarves and sunglasses in front of the deli.

"Yeah?"

"And that woman—she is her aunt. Last week, he goes up to them and hangs around the table, saying, 'How much are sunglasses? Do you have permit?' He's not the police, you know? He just wants to step on people's toes."

"I did hear that no one's allowed to sell on Seventh Avenue," I say.

"Yes. Last week, I got a ticket for a hundred and fifteen dollars."

"Jesus."

"And in my business, that's sort of part of the expenses, you know?"

"Sure."

"But it cuts into my profits."

"Yeah, that's lousy."

"The police—I didn't even see her coming. I was double parked and she snuck up behind me and cut a ticket."

"But you're here every week. She should know you by now."

"Yes. But she has a quota. The city makes millions from this parking ticket business."

"I didn't realize that they had a quota."

"The police, too. Yes. Everybody does."

Oskar and I look out through the open doors. The Mexican woman is wearing a black hat and black sweatshirt over a fuchsia tank top with jeans and black running shoes. She is wearing a tag around her neck that says, 'Vendor.'

"Well, at least she found good parking. She's right outside our doors. Heavy traffic. High volume," I say.

"Yes. She slept here overnight in her van," he says.

"I woke up late this morning. I went to bed at half past one and I woke up at five. I drove in from Astoria. I should've left earlier," he says with his hands at his waist, looking around.

"Every traffic light matters," Oskar says to me, looking at me square in the eyes.

"Otherwise, forget about finding parking." He shakes his head before sauntering slowly out the open doors with his hands at his sides. I wonder what it must be like to have your livelihood depend solely on good parking, which, in this city, is completely dependent on chance and luck.

A small white man with dark hair, mustache and glasses walks up to the counter.

"Excuse me, can I get some sai-rup?"

"Some syrup?"

"Ah, yes. Heh heh. See-rup."

69

Morning Beers

A black man in a red shirt enters. His neck is crooked to the right, his arms dangle on each side, his eyes are jaundiced, and his lower lip juts out. His baldhead shines beneath the fluorescent bulbs. His red shirt has white stains on the front and beneath the pits. He walks with a limp and drags his body over to the fridge at the back of the store. He stops in front of the beer section and stands there.

"That homeless guy. He want beer," Mr. Moy says to me.

"Yeah. He's thirsty."

Mr. Moy steps down from the platform and stands in the center of the floor with his arms crossed. The man walks back towards the front of the deli with a Budweiser tall boy in his hand.

"Excuse me," Mr. Moy says. The contorted man turns his body and looks at Mr. Moy. One of his eyes is white and faded.

"I cannot sell this to you right now. Today Sunday. You have to wait till twelve."

"Why not?"

"It illegal. It not twelve."

The man continues to walk towards the exit. Mr. Moy reaches for the can. The man turns his body the other way to keep it out of Mr. Moy's reach.

"C'mon. Give it back," Mr. Moy says. He's tired.

"Why? I'm just gonna go home and drink it. I'm just gonna take it home to drink it."

Mr. Moy looks at the man's face for a moment then slowly reaches for the beer behind the man's back. The man lets go.

"Fine! I wasn't even gonna drink it!" the man shouts, throwing his arms up in the air. He turns around and limps out of the deli, muttering something.

"It Sunday morning. Everybody wanna party righ now," says Mr. Moy.

The man staggers out. A white man wearing a white button down with "Amtrak" sewn above his shirt pocket walks in. He grabs two muffins, an orange juice, an oatmeal cookie, and a pack of gum. I ring them up.

"Nine seventy-five," I say. I put the items into a plastic bag. He hands me his credit card. I swipe and ask if he needs his receipt.

"No," he says.

"Sign please," I hand him the merchant's copy and pen. The man writes "2.00" on the tip line and signs.

"Thank you. Have a good one," I say.

I wave the receipt in my hand very hard. It shakes and flaps. Mr. Moy turns his head at the noise.

"You make tip?" he asks.

"I make tip!"

"How much?"

"Two dollars!"

"Whooooaa. That a lot of tip."

"I know. Amtrak guys always tip."

"Oh yeah?"

"Yes."

I punch in the invoice number into the credit card machine and adjust the total with the newly added tip. I pull a couple dollar bills from the register and stuff them into a Styrofoam cup. The tips add up. I eventually switch up all the coins and dollar bills for quarters before I leave the deli and use them to do my laundry.

Two men enter. Both are skinny and short. One of them is Latino with a small mountain of hair centered at the top of his head with the back and sides shaved. He's wearing a green T-shirt and a cut-up black sweatshirt. His partner is white with black-framed glasses, a black and white tank and jeans. The Latino guy tells the white guy something about people whose names are Melissa and Eric. They go straight to the back and grab two twenty-ounce bottles of Beck's and walk up to the register.

"I can't sell these to you right now," I tell them.

"What?! No. C'mon. We're going just down the block," says the Latino guy.

"I can't sell these before twelve. Blue law," I say.

"What?" says the white guy.

"Look. It's not like we're inspectors or anything. Do we look like inspectors to you?" says the Latino guy.

"No."

"Okay, then. Wrap 'em up. We'll pay for them."

"No."

"I know that they'll sell it to us up the street at that other deli," says the Latino guy.

"Then you can try over there."

The Latino guy makes a noise and grabs the white guy's elbow, leading him out of the store.

"We're not inspectors," says the white guy, turning to look at me over his shoulder while his boyfriend drags him out. I look at Mr. Moy. He shakes his head.

"They don't care if we get in trouble," says Mr. Moy.

The store carries ten different kinds of beers. Typically on a Sunday, a person who wants to continue the Saturday night boozing will walk straight to the fridge and look at the beers, deliberating over which one to choose in terms of both brand and size. The store has several sizes: twelve ounce, sixteen ounce, twenty-four ounce, and forty ounce. When the person finally grabs one and brings it to the register, I point at the clock and say something about the blue law and not selling before noon. Then the person usually tries to coax me into selling, and if I don't, the person resorts to anger. The current New York state law prohibits the sale of alcoholic beverages between three AM and noon on Sundays. I read somewhere that the blue law dates back to the Puritan days. The purpose of the law was to enforce religious morale among people on Sundays.

A white man with dark hair and a beard walks in. His eyes are red.

"Going for beer," Mr. Moy says to me.

"Yeah. He's smashed."

The man walks to the back, grabs a Budweiser tall boy and brings it to the register.

"Can't sell till noon," I say to him. The man immediately turns and leaves. I grab the tall boy and the bottles of Beck's back to the fridge. I return to the register.

70

Cream Cheese Bagel

A white teenaged boy with glasses, slightly curly brown hair, wearing a suit, tie, and black loafers drags his luggage in behind him.

"Excuse me, miss? How much is a bagel and a bottle of water?"

"A bagel with what on it," I ask.

"Cream cheese."

"A dollar seventy-five. A small bottle of Poland Spring is a dollar thirty-five."

"Okay," he says. He looks down at the floor for a second then looks up at me.

"May I have a bagel with cream cheese, please?" he asks.

"What kind of bagel?"

"Um…plain?"

"Toasted?"

"Yes, please."

"Cream cheese on toasted plain," I say to Mr. Moy.

"Toasted bagel with cream cheese," Mr. Moy calls back.

Donald walks in. He waves his hand at me and goes to Mr. Moy. Mr. Moy hands him a roll wrapped in wax-paper, which he brings over to the register.

"Ninety-five cents for you," I tell him.

"Hold on. Let me grab a coffee," he says, walking towards the coffee dispensers.

Mr. Moy hands me the toasted bagel wrapped in foil, marked "1.75" in black permanent ink. The boy drags his luggage behind him towards the register.

"Okay. One seventy-five for this and a buck thirty-five for the water. Total's three ten," I say.

The boy hands me three singles and a quarter. I return him the fifteen cents. The boy takes it then immediately puts out his hand.

"Is there a tip cup?" he asks. I stretch out my palm. He drops the coins.

"Thanks," I say. I bag the boy's items and look at a pin shaped like the American flag on his jacket collar. I look at another pin with green and gold leaves on it.

"Where you going," I ask.

"Washington."

"Model UN?"

"No. Youth in Government," he says.

"Does the UN run that?"

"No. YMCA does."

"Ah."

I tie up the bagged items and hand it to the boy.

"Are *you* in model UN?" the boy asks me. I grin.

"No," I say.

"Oh. Are you in high school?" he asks. I grin even wider. Donald stands behind the boy, shaking his head at the floor.

"No," I say.

"Oh. Sorry. You look like a senior in high school," says the boy. I grin and say nothing.

"College?" the boy asks.

"No," I say, handing him the paper bag with his bagel and napkins. "Have a good trip, sir."

"Oh. Thank you." The boy leaves.

Donald brings his roll, small coffee and two bananas to the register. I ring up the items and put the roll and bananas into a large, white paper bag. He hands me the money and I return his change.

Donald continues to shake his head.

"What?" I ask. He doesn't say anything. He takes the bag I hand him and walks out. He returns a second later and says,

"You cold. You cold," shaking his head.

Mr. Moy walks up to me.

"What happened?" he asks.

"I don't know. I think that little boy likes me," I say.

"Who? Cream cheese bagel?" he asks.

"Yeah."

Mr. Moy throws his head back and lets out a laugh.

71

Mr. Moy

Mr. Moy is fifty years old. He wears sneakers with white cotton socks, khaki shorts and a red T-shirt just like all the other deli employees. He has a round belly, a full head of hair and big teeth. He lives in Hoboken with his wife and sons and has been working at the deli for many years.

Mr. Moy moved to New Jersey in 1980 with his younger sister to join his parents in the US. Before that, he used to live in Guang Zho alone with his younger sister while his parents sent him money that they made at a plastics factory in Patterson.

"My parents sent me two-hundred dollars a month. That was a lot of money in China back then. I was living like a fucking king. Had a big house all to myself. I used to bring my friends, coworkers and girlfriends over to my house. We play mah-jong all night, smoke all night, and gamble."

When Mr. Moy moved to the US, he was twenty-years old. His aunt was already a naturalized American citizen by then and helping out Mr. Moy and his family obtain green cards. Knowing full well the hazards of factory work, Mr. Moy found a job at a restaurant supplies company that delivered and stocked inventory for Chinese restaurants on Canal Street. In the 1980s, the area teamed with young Vietnamese boys who worked part-time at restaurants during the day and ran with gangs at night. Mr. Moy 's Vietnamese delivery partner, Huy, drove the truck while smoking a joint. Huy also dealt drugs to make pocket cash on the side. Mr. Moy befriended a lot of Vietnamese guys his age and learned their language well enough to hold up conversations with Vietnamese girls, but he never touched their drugs. He said he didn't like them.

"When I was a boy in China, my cousin stayed with me at my house. He was addicted to cocaine and heroin. I remember he tried to quit one day. I was young, maybe ten. I was watching him shaking, throwing up, stuff dripping like faucet from the nose." Mr. Moy made a pulling motion with his hands coming from his lips with an expression like he was crying.

"I listen to him screaming. After that, I promise never to do drugs ever."

"That sounds scary."

"Yeah, sound scary! I was so young when I saw this, a little kid. Drugs scared me. But I know what marijuana smell like, ha ha."

"Yeah, I remember you asking me if I smelled marijuana last week, and I asked you how you knew what marijuana smells like. And you didn't say anything."

"Ha ha. I know. I know everything."

"Yeah. You're from the shits. Everybody here is from the shits. People from the shits know stuff."

72

Pablo's Beer

Pablo enters through the open glass doors and waves at me.

"Hi," he says.

"Hola, Pablo," I say.

Pablo heads over to the steam trays and walks around.

"So that Mexican guy finally sing for you?" Mr. Moy asks.

"Yes."

"I ask Pedro. Pedro say he sing like a maricon."

"He *is* a maricón. That's why I let him sing to me."

"Now you have love song singer for you," Mr. Moy says, walking back to the deli counter.

"Next," he says.

A middle-aged Latina woman asks him for a chicken panini. Pablo brings a small Styrofoam container of food and a beer.

"Pablo," I say. Pablo looks up at me. He has that same face that he always has—a half smile showing all his teeth, each tooth a gap apart from one another. He's wearing a white cowboy hat today. His long hair trails down his back in a ponytail. His eyes are big, dark and round. He looks real content.

"¿Qué hora es?" I ask.

Pablo looks down at his watch.

"Eleven fifteen," he says. I pick up the beer.

"So I cannot sell you this right now," I say.

"But today Saturday!" Pablo protests.

"Pablo, my man, today is not Saturday. See?" I raise the beer can and shake it in midair.

"You drink too many of these and now you think it's always Saturday," I say. A middle-aged white man standing behind Pablo chuckles and shakes his head.

"I'll bring it to you at twelve, okay?" I say.

"Okay." Pablo hands me a five. I return his change.

The white man places a small plastic container of string beans on the scale.

"He thinks it's Saturday?" he asks.

"Yeah. But he works hard."

"Yeah, I'll bet." The man accepts his change, takes his container of string beans and leaves.

"Next."

The middle-aged Latina woman brings her chicken panini wrapped in foil inside a plastic container.

"Seven thirty-five," I say.

"It says six ninety-five," she says, looking at me.

"Plus tax," I tell her.

The woman groans. She sets down her enormous tote bag on the freezer glass and starts searching for her wallet. I wait for fifteen seconds then look at the young black couple standing behind her.

"I'll take those for you," I say, taking their Styrofoam containers from their orange trays. I place them on the scale.

"Hey, wait!" the woman says. "I was here first. Hold *on* a minute!"

I weigh the young couple's items.

"Eighteen thirty-six," I tell the couple. The man hands me a twenty. I return his change. I place their items on an orange plastic tray with forks, knives, and napkins.

"Thank you."

The Latina woman finally hands me a ten. I return her change.

"You can't wait just two fucking minutes for me to find my wallet?" she says.

"I'm not gonna keep my customers waiting while you take forever to look for your wallet," I say.

"You are so rude. Who's your manager?"

"Take your food and get out of here."

The woman steps back to look me over.

"You're not gonna talk to me like that," she says.

"I'll talk to you however I want. Get the fuck out of here. Won't say it again."

"You are a bitch," she finally says, grabbing her container and walking towards the door.

The woman turns and disappears down the street.

Mr. Moy comes next to me.

"Okay, okay," he says. "Calm down, LJ. You're gonna scare away customer." He chuckles. I feel my hands shake.

"I'm gonna go give Pablo his beer now." I go to the fridge, pull a twelve-ounce can of Budweiser and bring it to Pablo.

"Beer, Pablo," I say. Pablo looks up at me then digs into his pocket. He hands me two singles.

"Gracias," he says.

73

A Letter

I grab a pen and a few pieces of blank sheets cut out from cigarette cartons that the staff uses as notepads. I take my moleskin notebook from under the counter then tell Mr. Moy that I'm taking a five-minute break before racing upstairs. I plop down at the nearest table and chair, and begin my letter to Daniel:

I'm so exhausted. I don't even wish to think or have a mind that functions anywhere outside of a mechanical means. Just calculate the total, hit the tax button, ask if people want their food to stay or to go... To stay or to go.

I really want to get far away from here and just have some time to figure out what I want to do with myself.

I realize that I've set myself up for an impossible situation, that is, I do not want a full-time corporate job. I feel as though that would kill me. But I do not want to go to school. That could just as easily kill me. I do not want to work at a restaurant anymore. That might kill me as well. I do not want to go to Korea. I do not want to continue doing what I am doing now. So what is there to do, really?

I guess I'll continue shopping around my manuscript of translations. I guess I'll keep writing my essays but I don't have the energy or the willpower to bring anything forward. I feel so drained right now.

'Why's living gotta be so hard?' Someone said that to me once. This guy I worked with at a restaurant said that to me in passing. I wish I knew the answer to that so that I can fix the problem and make living easier.

I felt bad after leaving your apartment so abruptly that day. I didn't know what else to say to you, but you didn't seem to want to say anything to me, either. Neither of us were committed to this. I don't suppose I'll even send this letter to you. We haven't even spoken since that morning.

I got to thinking lately about how I am incapable of any relationship whatsoever because I just don't know how to be good to others. Does that sound truthful to you? I'm not even sure if I am convinced by what I wrote just now.

I just know what I like at the time and will do anything to have it and then I'll stop…

I guess I'm just human. And I guess you are just human. We're just trying to figure out how to best pass the time.

Living is passing.

You were the main source of my happiness while I was in Seoul but nowadays it's a pain to be so far away from you, and have to struggle and fight against me wanting to be closer to you.

Timing is just not my friend. Not ever, it seems. None of the things that occurred to me in the last two years were timed well for me. I have to wonder how long this will keep up. When will time give up on me… or when will I give up on time and how to fit it into my context…?

Am I making any sense to you now?

My older friend Chuck gives me horrible advice on what to do with myself at my age. He says that I shouldn't waste away *my so-called best years. I hate him for saying things like that to my face but... I also feel pressured by my age, and what he tells me.*

Truth is, I don't want to do drugs or be a slut (this is what he is advising me with). I don't want to be destructively happy. I want to be honest and hardworking, and construct something real and meaningful with my time. How can I be that way? And how can I get there? Do you understand me?

I want to feel unbounded by anyone. I don't want to feel like there's a person looming over me to approve or disapprove of my life. I just want to be the judge of me. But how can I be that way without cutting off the world? And why is it such a struggle for me to face myself and how I am?

I wish you were here right now. I feel like if you were next to me, all of these thoughts would shut down, and I would stop feeling so nervous and anxious—so down and out. I think if you were here we could just go for a walk and see interesting things around us and talk about them.

I stop writing for a second. I open my moleskin and find a folded sheet of paper with an ink drawing of a house. Hot tears sting the back of my eyes.

Hope to see you soon.

-LJ

74

Big Phil

"Heeeeeeeeey, Big Philly," I say. Phil smiles at me.

"How are you doing, gorgeous?" he asks. He drops a pizza box off at the deli counter.

"Chicken and broccoli. For you, LJ," he says.

"Thanks honey."

A fat, white man with red hair, no shoes and no teeth enters the deli. He walks over to the salad bar, and stands over the food, staring at the fruit and lettuce. A couple of women in saris look at him and back away.

Mr. Moy looks back in concern.

Phil walks over to the man.

"Excuse me. You need to leave," he says to him.

"Why? I'm gonna buy something."

"Then buy something. But I know you not gonna buy anything. You stole from the gyro and pizza place next door. I know you."

The man stands directly in front of Phil and screams,

"Get off my back you stupid nigger! You're a fucking nigger!"

"Get out of here," Phil says.

The man starts laughing. He slowly drags his body out of the deli.

"Phil. You alright?" I ask.

"Just doing my job, sweetie."

75

"Oye, Armando."

"Sí."

"What are you doing tomorrow?"

"Day off."

"What are you gonna do?"

"No se. Sueño."

"Sleep?"

"Sí."

I tap on the lemon slice and pull out a few plastic bags. I air them out and pile them on top of the counter.

"What's your immigration status, Armando?"

"Heh heh."

"Aaaahhh. It's OK. I won't tell." I bring a finger to my lips.

"Heh heh."

"How many niños you have?"

"Niños?"

"Yeah."

"Tres."

I hold up three fingers.

"Tres?!" I ask.

"Si."

"Where do they go to school?"

"South Bronx."

"How old are your kids?"

"Mm. The oldest twelve. The other one seven. Another one five."

"Where do they go to school? P.S. what?"

"Um… P.S. forty six."

"Ah, OK."

I raise the volume on my iPod. The song's a Cat Power cover of "Angelitos Negros." I hear the words "todo" and "siempre." I look at Armando. He stares at the clock, looking like he's either deep in thought or not thinking about a thing.

"Armando," I say.

Armando looks at me and starts smiling.

"What does 'todo' mean?"

"Todo?"

"Yes."

"Todo means 'all.'"

"What does 'siempre' mean?"

"Siempre means 'always.'"

76

Avatar

Donald from Hotel Pennsylvania enters.

"Container of fruit for you, righ?" Mr. Moy says. Donald salutes Mr. Moy. Mr. Moy tells him that his dreadlocks look like the hair on the blue people in *Avatar*.

"But you know what those blue people in that movie are, right?" Donald says. Mr. Moy doesn't say anything.

"They're black," I say.

Donald points at me and says, "See? She knows."

He walks to the back of the store laughing hysterically. A minute later, he returns with a small container of fruit and a piece of bread to the register. I punch numbers into the register and bag the items.

"How much?" he asks.

"Four thirty-seven," I say. I hand him the bag.

"Did you think I was mean to that kid this morning?" I ask.

"What do you think?" he asks, widening his eyes.

"Don't think I was."

"See, that's the problem with you women. Y'all are cold and don't even know it," Donald says.

"That kid is ten years younger than I am," I say.

"So? Don't you know nature?" Donald asks.

"What?"

"Someday you might be married to that kid!" Donald says. I laugh. Donald waves his hand dismissively and leaves.

"What did he say?" Mr. Moy asks me, pulling off his rubber gloves.

"Doesn't matter."

I step down from the platform and walk around a bit. I stretch my legs and let out a high-pitched yawn. Mr. Moy laughs at me and asks if I ever heard Arnold's yawn before.

"Yes," I say.

"Yeah. He sound like dinosaur, righ?"

77

Cop

A broad-shouldered white NYPD officer steps in. He goes to the salad bar, fills a small clear container with cantaloupe, strawberries and honeydew. He grabs a tray and fills a large Styrofoam container with French fries, turkey breast and Brussels sprouts. He brings the tray to the register.

"To go," he tells me, looking down at his wallet. He hands me a five.

I look at him and say, "The total is twelve seventy-five."

"What?" he asks.

Mr. Moy comes over to the register.

"This guy always pay five dollars. He have a deal with Mr. Choi."

"Oh. Ok."

I bag the items and hand the cop the bag.

"Have a good one, officer."

"Bye now."

The cop leaves.

"Mr. Moy, how come that guy gets away with five dollars?"

"Mr. Choi and that cop have a deal. Something with parking. Mr. Choi can park in front of the deli anytime and that cop don't cut him any tickets."

"Oh-h-h-h. That's corrupt."

"Well. That's what Mr. Choi do for business. Most cop don't care. That cop has a good deal."

"Yeah, I guess."

78

Comb, Toothbrush, Toothpaste and Razor

A Latino man of average height and glasses stands in front of the register.

"Excuse me," he says. "Do you have…?" He starts to brush his hair with an invisible hairbrush. I turn around and pull out a plastic container full of small black combs. There are fifty combs in the container. Each comb is sold for a dollar each.

"Yes," I say. I show him the black comb.

"Do you have big one?" he asks.

"No. This is all we got."

"Okay. Can I have…what you call this?" He grins widely at me, revealing his teeth, and starts to brush them with an invisible toothbrush. I turn and grab a toothbrush from the shelf behind me.

"Okay. What I want is…" He starts squeezing invisible toothpaste across the head of the invisible toothbrush he's still holding in his hand. I turn around and pull a small tube of Colgate from the shelf. I set it down on the counter and slide it towards him.

"How do you call this?" he asks me, picking up the toothpaste.

"Toothpaste," I say.

"Toose-pace," he says. I pick up the toothbrush and say, "Toothbrush."

"Okay. I don't want," he says, waving the toothbrush away and looking down at his wallet for cash.

"Do you have…uh…?" He starts to shave his face with an invisible razor, moving his mouth from left to right as the invisible razor touches each cheek, and raising his chin up while looking straight at me, as if my face were his reflection. I turn around and pull out a disposable Gillette razor from a box.

"Okay! Thank you. How much?"

79

Lunch Rush

It's the lunch rush. People are entering in droves. The hot trays and salad bar are swarmed. Armando and Mr. Moy are taking orders and shouting them back out to confirm. The line gets long. This is the best time. My mind turns off and I only watch my hands move. I hear my voice calling out the numbers that appear on the register screen. I take the people's cash and return change. When I see a number on the register, my hands already know which compartment in the register I need to reach into to make the correct change: Two dollars for a dollar sixty means forty cents in change; by the time I realize it, my hands are already putting together a quarter, nickel and dime; when a customer hands me a sandwich on a round roll with Armando's handwriting that reads, "4.99," I already know to just punch in "5.43" into the register, skipping the TAX button. I swipe cards and pull out their receipts for signature while handing an outstretched hand a pen. It feels good to finally get busy again after a few hours of just watching flies buzz around the fluorescent bulbs.

When I am actually still, what makes the deli unbearably depressing is its constant reminder of routine. Routine. It is unending routine. Price tags, the exchange of cash or credit, the bagging, the moving. And the patrons at the deli are just as caught up in the routine as the employees. They stand in lines, they know how to grab a tray, they know to move it along so that the person behind them can get to where they're going. The activity here is a reminder of the endlessness and pointlessness of routine. When people walk in here, they're not here to catch up with old friends or enjoy the ambience. It is filthy here. They just come in, grab whatever looks good enough to dismiss their hunger then go right back out there, onto whatever's next.

A white woman brings a Styrofoam container and places it on the scale. I punch the numbers into the register and hit the TAX button. The total number appears on the screen.

"Fourteen forty-nine," I say. I grab a plastic bag and air it out.

"To stay or to go?" I ask.

"To go."

I grab a rubber band and seal the Styrofoam container. I grab a couple of napkins and wrap a fork and knife around it. All items go into the plastic bag I just aired out, and the handles get tied into a single knot. I look up and see that the woman is still digging for pennies in her tiny coin pouch.

She retrieves three and opens her palm out to me. She already wasted enough of my time and I can feel my consciousness returning to the deli space. I want her to leave. She's not worth the extra penny, the extra discussion, the extra wait.

"That's good. Have a nice day." The bag gets handed to her. "Next!"

Mr. Moy hands me a Kaiser roll wrapped in white paper.

"Four ninety-nine," he tells me.

"Four ninety-nine," I repeat.

A Jamaican woman limps into the store. She asks me for the restroom key. I turn to my left and look for the key, attached to an eight-by-two inch block of wood wrapped in duct tape. It usually rests on top of the deli glass, but isn't there anymore.

"Someone must be using it right now. But you can check upstairs," I tell her. "No key."

"Upstairs? But my calf is painin' me," she says.

"Sorry. Don't know what to tell ya," I say. I stretch my hand out towards a very short, young Latina girl with bored eyes and a ponytail. She places a small plastic carton of chicken, rice, and avocadoes on the scale.

"Upstairs…" the Jamaican woman repeats to herself. "I can't go up there."

I tap on the register screen that reads "$5.48" and look at the small girl. She digs through her purse.

"Where is the restroom upstairs?" the Jamaican woman asks.

"Upstairs," I repeat loudly. I point to the back of the store. "You go up those stairs and make a right and you'll see a bathroom."

"Oh, no. It's too far." The Jamaican woman limps and turns around to leave.

I look down at the girl. She doesn't say anything to me but continues to look at me with her bored eyes. I tap on the screen again.

"Five forty eight," I tell her.

She hands me four rolled up singles. I unwrap them and run my finger across the back of the bills to bend them slightly at the center.

"What are you waiting for, sweetheart," I say to the girl. She shrugs her shoulders.

"No ing-gleesh," she says to me.

"Well, these aren't English," I say to her, tapping on the screen. A fat thirty-something-year-old white man in checkered shorts stands behind the girl and tries to get my attention. I point at the register across from me and say, "Someone will help you at that register, sir."

The man says, "Oh" and walks towards the other register where Mr. Moy bags a couple of sixteen-ounce soda bottles into a plastic bag for a white girl with blue and silver dreadlocks tied back with purple band.

I wait. The girl continues to look at me with her bored eyes.

"If you need an ATM, there's one right next door at McDonald's," I say to her. She shrugs her shoulders again. I let out a huff. She points her finger at the dollar bills in my hand.

"Gimme," she says. I hand her the bills. The girl walks out, leaving behind her carton of food. I toss the carton aside on the deli counter.

The line gets longer. I look up and see the man with the contorted body and red shirt—the one who tried to buy a Budweiser tall boy this morning. He slowly makes his way towards the people standing in line, one by one.

"Excuse me, spare some change? Sir? Excuse me, miss, do you have some change?" The people stand in line with their eyes fixed straight ahead. A man shakes his head slowly without making eye contact with the man with the contorted body.

I look up.

"Ay!"

The man slowly turns his body around to face me.

"Leave my customers alone."

"I'm not even doing anything!" the man yells.

"If you're gonna bother my customers for money and not buy anything then get out of here."

The next customer brings her tray to the counter—a white woman with orange hair and green earrings. She places each item down onto the counter, one by one: water, muffin, apple, chips, and a Snickers bar. She smiles at me nervously.

"Well, you're not even born here!" the contorted man yells.

I ring up the woman's items. She hands me a twenty. I press the register and the cash drawer pops out.

"I'm an American! You're not even from here. I was born here. You're not even from here! Get out of my country! You Chinese motherfucker!" the contorted man continues to yell.

I bag the items up and hand them to the white woman.

"Next!"

A middle-aged white man with headphones brings chips, bottled water and two long roll sandwiches to the register.

"Go back to China! You're not even American!" the contorted man shouts again.

I look up at the white man. He looks back at me for a second then looks down at the food items.

"Twenty-one seventy-five," I say to him. He hands me his credit card. I swipe.

"Need your receipt?"

"No. Thanks."

"Sign please." I hand him the merchant copy and a pen. He signs.

"Thank you. Next!"

The contorted man limps out of the deli.

A tall black man with glasses and a backpack leaves the line and exits the deli. A second later, he returns with the contorted man trailing behind him. The tall man turns his head around and asks the contorted man, "Ay, whatchu want? Ham and cheese? Turkey?"

"Ham and cheese," says the contorted man quietly.

"My man, lemme get two ham cheese sandwiches on a long roll with lettuce and tomato. Make it American cheese," the tall man tells Mr. Moy.

"Two ham and cheese," Mr. Moy responds and gets to work on the sandwiches.

"My friend, you want anything else? You want chips and soda or anything?" the tall man asks.

"No. No. Just the sandwich," the contorted man replies.

A couple of minutes pass. The line dwindles.

The tall man is at the register. The contorted man stands behind him, swaying from left to right, shifting the weight on his feet.

"Hey miss, I'm sorry about that. Excuse my man right here. He didn't mean nothing," the tall man says to me. "How much for the sandwiches and the waters here?"

I ring him up. I skip the TAX button.

"Seventeen forty-eight," I tell him. "Don't worry about the tax."

I bag up his items and hand him the bag.

"Hey, thanks a lot miss. You have a beautiful day now."

Outside the deli doors, I see the tall man hand the contorted man a bottle of water and a sandwich.

"Thank you," the contorted man says.

"Alright. You take care now. You take care of yourself." The tall man turns around and joins the crowd as he leaves, walking north as the contorted man turns and heads down south.

80

Madison Square Garden Security Guard

"To stay or to go?!" the old white man shouts as he walks in. He is one of the security guards at Madison Square Garden. He is seventy something years old. He's overweight, has white hair, slumped shoulders and a red, pockmarked face, and a large red nose with a knob at the end. Booze nose. He moves very slowly but walks with quick, little steps, slouching, and his heavy face droops down. I've never seen him smile before.

"To stay or to go?!" he shouts again, looking at me. I smile at him.

"Yeah, to stay or to go?" Mr. Moy says to him from behind the deli counter. Mr. Moy laughs. The old man goes to the steam trays.

"His eye is better," Mr. Moy says to me.

"Yeah."

Last week, the old man came in with a crusty red wound right above his eye that was patched up with gauze. I wanted to ask him about it but didn't. The first time I ever encountered him, I asked him what I ask every customer: "To stay or to go?" and he responded by looking back at me with his dull, tired blue eyes and said,

"Where am I gonna take it?" Then Mr. Moy came over to me and said,

"No, no, this guy come here everyday. He stays." The old man asked me again,

"Where am I gonna take it?" I didn't say anything. At the time, I wasn't sure if I liked him or hated him.

The old man brings a container of lo mein, roasted potatoes with crushed red pepper, string beans and chicken. I weigh the container on the scale then punch the total into the register

"Fourteen sixty," I say.

I place the container on an orange tray alongside some napkins, a fork and a knife. The old man hands me a twenty. I hit the ALT button on the register and pull out his change. Mr. Moy walks over and stands beside us.

"Working on Sunday?" Mr. Moy asks the old man.

"Yup!"

"Why you never talk but I always see you talking on the phone?"

"Yup!"

"You never talk."

"Yup!"

"Work on Sunday, you make a lot of money. A lot of money, good, right?"

"Yeah. I'm loaded. I'll lose some of it when I go to the bathroom," says the old man.

"Yeah…."

The old man takes the tray from the counter, turns and walks to the seating area.

"Yup!" he shouts.

I watch as he walks away. The back of his white button down, short-sleeve shirt says, 'SECURITY' in black letters.

Mr. Moy turns to me, "I feel bad for him. He should not be working. He so old! How he gonna chase down somebody? That guy so fucking fat and old, how he gonna catch somebody if they robbing?"

Mr. Moy shakes his head and continues, "I ask him about his eye last week, and he say, 'If I say that I fell down, will you believe me?' I think his daughter hit him. He came in a couple years ago with a black eye, look like fucking raccoon or something. He say his daughter hit him because she want money."

I look at the old man from the deli platform. He's sitting at a table, closest to the wall. I watch him as he eats. He's wearing a tie. He has white hair. He puts chicken into his mouth and chews without looking up. He keeps looking down at his food. He eats very slowly. Eating looks like a chore to him.

I once dated a guy in college who said that he hated eating. He said that eating seemed like a waste of time and money. He didn't understand why our bodies functioned in such an inefficient way. He didn't understand why we had to buy food because we were hungry or why we had to eat only to shit it out later. Then we broke up and I started seeing someone who didn't think that eating was such a big waste of time but one of the many pleasures in life.

Working at a deli, though, eating doesn't seem like a pleasure. It seems a chore, like people just eat because they need to satisfy a need. They're not interested in what's innovative, or flavors that work but haven't been tried out before. They have no interest in the aesthetics of a cuisine.

Their sole interest is in something just good enough to satiate them fast. The kinds of food that get sold at a deli are not very healthy. Working weekends while watching others who work weekends come in during their lunch breaks only makes me wonder what the point of this all is. Working just because we get hungry and need to afford money to eat only to shit it out later. It also makes me ask if it couldn't be any better than this.

I remember that bit in Hamsun's *Hunger*, when the starving narrator finally manages to get some beef. He eats it all in one sitting only to barf it out later. He complains of how impoverished he is, and how he's so poor that he can't even manage to buy a book when he feels completely hopeless. The character is very real and very stupid and very intelligent all at once.

"You want eat anything?" Mr. Moy asks. "You want ice cream?"

"I'm gonna take a walk," I say.

"Okay. Go, take a walk. Go have a smoke or something."

"Okay," I say.

I grab a small white plastic bag from under the register and toss in the small plastic container of food that the small bored Latina girl had left behind. I throw in a fork, tie the bag up and walk out. The temperature outside is no different from the temperature inside by the register counter. Since the register is closest to the door, the customers often walk in complaining about how hot it is. I tell them to go sit in the back where the air conditioning is stronger.

I light a cigarette and wander through the crowd. I see a couple of tour bus ticket men in their red vests talking to each other. One of them looks at me. I wave. He nods his head and continues to speak to his friend. I cross the street towards Madison Square Garden. There's a bum sitting in front of a rose bush with multiple layers of clothing on. He is sleeping. I leave the plastic bag next to him and walk into the Borders bookstore. I browse over the bestseller's table then wander over to the fiction section. I make my way towards the door and catch a glimpse of the bearded guy who drinks Sam Adams at the deli.

81

Price Gun and Cigarettes

Right around three o'clock the store gets real slow. Everybody's heads are buzzing with their own separate thoughts. Nobody's talking anymore. People look at one another straight in the eye and yawn.

I walk around and touch boxes of cookies. I go behind the deli glass and look under the shelves. I pull out a price tag gun. I raise it in the air and show it to Mr. Moy.

"That thing is broke," he says.

"What is it?"

"Price gun. Here, I show you."

Mr. Moy pulls the orange roll of labels to fit the lip of the label dispenser.

"You set the price here. See the number? This one here is dolla. This one here is cent. So set to four ninety-nine."

Mr. Moy hands the gun to me. I swipe the price gun against Mr. Moy 's arm.

"I'm four ninety-nine, eh?" he asks.

"Just be glad you're not *three* ninety-nine."

Mr. Moy laughs.

I walk to the back of the store and raise a bag of chips in the air.

"How much are the Cape Cod Chips?" I ask.

"That has price on it already. We don't use the price gun anymore. That thing broke."

I walk back to the deli glass and put the price gun back underneath the shelf. The real reason why we don't use the price gun anymore is because the prices at the deli change unpredictably. Suddenly one weekend, all the boxed dry foods cost an extra twenty-five cents and it just doesn't seem worth it to retag all the boxes with new prices.

"Go outside. Have smoke," Mr. Moy says.

"Nah—I don't want to."

"How old were you when you start smoking?"

"Eighteen. My boyfriend at the time was a smoker."

"Oh—so, you start smoking cause you watch and learn from your boyfriend, huh?"

"Well, my dad was also a heavy smoker for a while."

"Ah—yeah. See? Kids learn after watching from parents. That's why I started. Cause I see my parents, righ? They light—" Mr. Moy pretends to light a cigarette, "—and they blow smoke—" he blows imaginary smoke into the air, "and it look so cool. Look like magic, you know?" he smiles.

"When did you start smoking?" I ask.

"Oh-h-h-h. Long time. I started when I was fourteen or fifteen. Yeah, my father and grandfather had the... the..." Mr. Moy makes a gesture with his hands like he is rolling something.

"Loose tobacco," I say.

"Yeah. Loose tobacco, and make me roll cigarettes on rolling machine. They make me get them forty or fifty cigarettes, so I take three or four and put them in my pocket, heh heh."

"Ha ha."

"And no filter! So I smoke, I get dizzy, and I smoke all the time after. But I quit ten years ago."

"Good for you, man."

"Yeah. Sometime I think, ah… maybe I try one. But nah—I quit and it's good."

82

Todo es Para Siempre

A Latina woman and her husband bring two Styrofoam containers to the register. They are having a heated discussion, rapid-firing Spanish and not looking at me. They place the containers on the orange trays. I take each container and weigh it on the scale.

"Todo?" I ask the woman.

"Sí," the woman says.

I place the items on the orange trays. I put out napkins and utensils and say,

"Twenty three seventy seven."

The woman stops speaking to her husband and pulls out her wallet.

"Cuando?" she asks. I point at the numbers on the register screen. The woman leans in and looks.

"Okay." She hands me a twenty and three singles, then places a quarter on the scale and slides it towards me. She places a nickel on the scale and slides it towards me. She pulls out a dime and raises it to my face asking, "Cuando?"

"That's ten," I tell her. I drag the quarter towards me and say, "And that's vente cinco."

I reach for the nickel saying, "That's cinco."

"You gave me quarenta. I need seventy-seven cents," I tell her.

The woman gives me three quarters and seven pennies, leaving the change on the scale. She takes one tray and her husband takes the other. They go to the back and sit.

83

Mexican Vendor

The Mexican vendor lady just outside the deli doors says something to her niece then enters.

"Excuse me, you have key to bathroom?" she asks.

"Yeah." I grab the key and hand it to her.

"Gracias."

"Of course."

I look outside and see her niece standing behind the vendor table. She has long dark hair that she ties up in a ponytail. She's wearing an orange tank top and jeans. She moves the items around on the table with her long, skinny arms whenever people stop to look at sunglasses. She looks about sixteen. The Mexican vendor lady returns with the key.

"Thank you," she says to me.

"You've been here all night?" I ask.

"Since four," she says to me, rolling her eyes.

"That's rough. Come in anytime you need to use the toilet. Come and have coffee, too, if you want. Tell your niece the same," I tell her.

"Oh, thank you, thank you, honey." The woman smiles at me then leaves. Mr. Moy walks up beside me.

"That woman use bathroom?" he asks.

"Yeah. She was here overnight. Parked outside."

"That's cause over there good parking here on Sunday. Free," he says.

"Do they need permits to sell here?"

"Actually they not suppose to sell on Seventh Avenue. They only suppose to sell on Thirty-fourth Street."

"So I can blackmail them?"

"Yeah. Tell them you call police if they don't give you discount on hat."

"Ha ha."

"I'm no joke! Go say, 'Gimme one hat or I call police.' And they give you hat. Take two if you want."

"Fine. I'll do that."

I look back out the open doors and see the Mexican vendor woman and her niece cover the table with a large black plastic bag.

"O-h-h-h," says Mr. Moy looking at me. "I think police go over there."

84

Cheesecake

Big Phil is taking a break from the fast food restaurants next door. He walks over to the cappuccino machine and fills a twenty-ounce paper cup full of hot chocolate.

"Digging the instant mix, Phil?" I ask.

"Just craving something sweet," he tells me.

"Phil, you lost weight," I say, grinning.

"Thanks. I can't get any bigger." Phil walks over to Gelato Girl and says hello. He returns to the register.

Mr. Moy walks over.

"Hey, Phil! LJ want some chicken broccoli pizza today."

"Chicken broccoli, eh?" asks Phil. "You just ate one today, didn't you?"

"Yeah. I'm stuffed." I say.

"No. She a big girl. This girl can *eat*," says Mr. Moy. "Go get her another one chicken broccoli pizza."

Pedro walks over to Mr. Moy with a plate of something.

"It's for LJ," Pedro says. "From downstairs," he says.

I look. It's a cheesecake.

"Oh-h-h-h… It somebody birthday?" Mr. Moy asks.

"Sí. Naniel," Pedro says then walks away.

I grab a fork and dig into the cheesecake.

"Cheesecake… Man. That's the killer, man," says Phil.

"You want a bite, Philly?" I ask.

"No. I am good. I'll go get you your pizza now," he says as he turns to leave. Mr. Moy starts to laugh. Big Phil turns around and laughs with him.

85

Eating Fast

The skinny Chinese man who works next door at Chinatown Express carries in a Styrofoam container of beef and rice. He wears glasses, and he always hands me two singles as soon as he walks in, in the morning to pay for the two bagels he is about to order while talking to Mr. Moy in Mandarin.

Mr. Moy says something to the guy and the guy waves at him then waves at me before leaving. I watch Mr. Moy eat. He mechanically shovels food into his mouth. It's as though all the lights in the deli has been shut off and it's just him and the container of beef and rice.

I look at the row of yogurt cups across from me and wonder if I should make parfaits later. A minute later, I hear the Styrofoam container get tossed into the trash. I look back and see Mr. Moy wiping his mouth with a napkin.

"Wow," I say.

"Ha ha. Yeah, I eat fast. I don't know why. You what it is," Mr. Moy says, raising his hand in the air, pointing at something in his memory, "it's because after high school, they send us to learn the, uh..." Mr. Moy starts hoeing an imaginary field with an invisible hoe, "...to learn the fucking farming. So stupid. After high school they send us to farm." Mr. Moy laughs.

"There I learn how to gamble and do all that fucking thing,

ha ha. But when we eat, we *eat*. You sit down and everybody," Mr. Moy starts to make a chow-down impression, digging up invisible food from an invisible plate and shoving the invisible spoon into his mouth. I start laughing.

"All the food. Gone," Mr. Moy has his hands out to his sides, like he is asking, "What the fuck?" He looks at me as if he is asking me the same question, pausing in his story.

"It's like you turn around and back and the food, all gone. So if you don't hurry up and eat, you'll be hungry. So that's why I eat so fast."

86

Twenty-five Hours a Day, Eight Days a Week

A teenaged white girl with blonde hair wearing pink cotton shorts and a Jets jersey walks over to the register.

"What time you close?"

"Never," I say.

The girl gives me a confused look.

"We never close," says Mr. Moy, walking over to the register, waving his hand to emphasize 'never.'

"Oh," she says. The girl leaves.

"Yeah, when do we close?" I ask.

"We never close. We open twenty-five hour a day, eight day a week," Mr. Moy says. "On September eleven, the police came and said we all needed to leave the store and get out. But we cannot lock the door. That door—go look at it—it never lock. It have no lock. We leave the store so somebody come take all the money from the register? Or steal from store?"

"We cannot leave the register. There was one girl working other register over there. She from Santa Domingo. She get phone call say World Trade Center get hit by plane. But I thought, you know, maybe some fucking helicopter or something. I don't believe her. Police come and say leave because maybe the bomb come hit Madison Square Garden or Penn Station. Or if they hit Empire State building, big problem here. So they tell us to leave the store." Mr. Moy pauses for a second, looking at me.

"September eleven, lots of bomb scare. Everywhere bomb threat calling. Everywhere," Mr. Moy says.

"The deli has no locks cause it never closes?"

"It never close."

"Christmas?"

"Christmas, it never close. Remember black out?"

"Yeah."

"On blackout, we were only store open. We no have lights so we use flash light to go downstair." Mr. Moy starts to smile. "No light. But we no close."

"Open even on September eleven," I say.

"That's why I say it open twenty-five hour, eight day a week."

87

Kids Conspiring

"I'll be right back," I tell Mr. Moy.

"Okay."

I go upstairs and into the bathroom. The ladies' room upstairs has two stalls. One of them does not lock properly. I take a leak, wash my hands with foaming soap and warm water. I like washing my hands at the deli. I think about all the money, food, and counter space that I touched while washing, then watch it all go down the drain as grey, soapy water.

Outside of the restroom, I push some chairs in back under the table around the dining area. I overhear some kids talking. A white boy, about fifteen years old, wearing glasses and a hat, and two girls, a redhead and a blonde chat casually.

"I could say that there's hair in this food, and if they say that it's my hair, I'll just say that it can't be," says the boy.

"Okay," the blonde says.

I walk downstairs, past the salad bar and return to my register.

"Mr. Moy, I just listened to some kids conspiring. Just a heads-up."

Mr. Moy takes a box of oatmeal cookies from a tall white man's hand and drops it into a small plastic bag.

"Okay," he says.

A large black woman brings two enormous Styrofoam containers and places them on the scale.

"Total comes to forty-three fifty-two," I say.

"Damn!" the woman cries. She pulls her leather purse in front of her and pulls out her wallet.

"Forty something dollars for this much food? I didn't even get that much!" the woman says. She widens her eyes at me in disbelief. They are fixated on me. I say nothing and hold out my hand as she drops a credit card into it. I swipe.

"Receipt?" I ask.

"Of *course*," she says. "Damn."

I push "yes" to "Customer Copy."

"Sign, please," I say. I set down a pen and the two receipts in front of her. She signs the merchant copy and hands it back to me.

I put rubber bands around the two containers and place them into a large plastic bag. I throw in two forks, knives and some napkins then tie the bag into a knot.

"Thank you," I say. The woman leaves. I look up and see Mr. Moy looking at the kids who were conspiring upstairs. The boy with the glasses says,

"This isn't my hair. I want my money back."

Mr. Moy doesn't say anything. The blonde girl puts her arm around the boy's arm as the redhead looks on. She leans over to one side, shifting most of her weight to her left leg.

"Well, because you finished eating most of it, I cannot refund you your money," Mr. Moy explains. Then he calls for the next customer.

"Next." An old white man shuffles over to the register. He has patches of brown spots all over his bald head. His blue eyes have a white film over them, and he stares out intensely, like he can't really see what's in front of him. He concentrates very hard at everything he looks at. His back is hunched over. He's wearing flannel slacks, a brown suit jacket, and brown loafers.

"To stay," he says. He sets down a plastic container of mashed potatoes, peas and carrots on the scale.

"Four ninety-five," says Mr. Moy.

"How much?" he asks.

"Four ninety-five," Mr. Moy repeats.

The old man hands him a five. Mr. Moy returns a nickel, set down napkins, a fork and knife and spoon on the orange tray, and hands him the tray. The kids stand there and talk amongst themselves until they finally leave.

88

Yankees vs. Blue Jays

A fly buzzes around the long fluorescent tubes in the ceiling. A still summer air hangs about the register. Far in the back are two patrons silently eating their food alone at separate tables. They're both looking down.

"I'm bored," I say.

Mr. Moy takes out a small battery powered radio from behind a large box of matches. He turns it to ESPN. Yankees versus Toronto.

"What's the score?" I ask.

"Two to zero, Toronto."

"Fuck."

"It's okay. Still first inning."

A white guy in his late twenties walks into the deli. He is wearing black-framed glasses, jeans and a green V-neck T-shirt. He has large black headphones wrapped around his neck and David Foster Wallace's *Infinite Jest* tucked under his armpit. He grabs a can of Red Bull and brings it over to the register.

"Four dollars," I tell him.

The guy pulls out four crumpled bills from his pocket. He fumbles with them, flattening the bills out with his hands as the enormous book wobbles around inside the space between his arm and torso.

"How's Wallace treating you?"

"He's a great writer," says the guy. "He's such an important writer." He rests the book on top of the register, flattening each bill one by one.

"Okay. Four dollars."

The guy hands the bills to me. He brings his hands to his headphones and raises them up to his ears. I look at his face. His eyes are a bit slant. There's harshness to his face, like whatever lies deeper inside of him isn't quite accessible.

"Bye. Happy reading," I say.

The guy doesn't reply. He looks down at his iPhone and walks out the door. He has an awkward walk, like he is walking on stilts. He probably moved to Brooklyn not too long ago. Maybe from Pennsylvania or something.

A middle-aged black man enters the deli. He looks really tired. He goes to the back of the deli, grabs a bottle of Poland Spring and brings it to Mr. Moy's register.

"One thirty-five," says Mr. Moy. The man freezes and stares at Mr. Moy.

"Yesterday your man charged me a dollar fifty for this. What is that?"

"It's a dollar thirty-five," says Mr. Moy.

"I'm only giving you a dollar twenty for this here."

Mr. Moy doesn't say anything. He accepts the man's bill and change.

"You people are grimy," the man says before turning around to leave.

Mr. Moy turns to me: "You know, some of the Korean guys charge black people dollar fifty on some days, so they come in and give me hard time."

"That's a shame," I say.

"Yeah."

Mr. Moy has two sons. They both go to Rutgers University. One is studying to become an accountant. The other is studying to become a pharmacist. Mr. Moy became naturalized as a citizen on his forty-fifth birthday. When I ask him why he doesn't try to get a better job where it's not as hard on him physically, he laughs and says he's too old to switch jobs right now, and that he's comfortable with this routine nowadays. A few weeks ago, Meeja had surgery on her leg because some idiot hit her with his car while she was crossing the street. The doctor told her not to stand on her feet all day but Meeja still came into work five days a week and stood on both legs for ten hours. When I asked her why she doesn't take time off she asked me in return,

"Who's going to man the register? Who's going to pay the bills at home?"

The deli offers no health insurance. It doesn't offer sick days or vacation days. If you're out, you're out. If you need health insurance, you buy it out of pocket. Both Meeja and Mr. Moy are naturalized citizens but neither have proper health care. Same goes for me. It's hard to say it doesn't make me nervous but what can we do? This is our reality.

The lack of basic human resources at the deli amazes me. Every little thing is so heavily dependent on the other without any room for contingency. If one thing falls through, everything's fucked. If one person is out, people panic. The rent at the deli is fifteen thousand dollars a month. In twelve hours, the register is expected to make somewhere between thirteen and fifteen hundred. Anything less would ruin everything; the boss will have to make cuts just to make the rent.

I look up and see a little kid crying. He walks away from the rows and rows of candy bars and gum. His mother puts out her hand and says, "Come here," very softly. The kid walks over to her. She wraps her arm around his shoulders then walks out the door with her son.

89

Last Day

LJ sat down on a ledge beneath a tree just outside of Gwanghwamun station in front of the bookstore. She looked up ahead and saw Daniel emerging from the subway station. She waved at him.

"Been waiting long?" he asked.

"No."

LJ and Daniel boarded a green bus. They sat in the back. LJ leaned her head against Daniel's shoulder and shut her eyes.

"I can't sleep," she said.

"Then sit up properly. We're almost there."

LJ and Daniel got off at the stop. They walked up a path that led them up a mountain. They looked down at the small apartment buildings' rooftops. There were ceramic kimchi storage pots and green plants everywhere. LJ and Daniel walked back down towards the street, and down a staircase that led them into a narrow alleyway—a concrete hill slanted downwards with walls of two buildings on each side. LJ walked carefully down in small steps as Daniel walked on ahead. A minute later he stopped and waited for her to catch up. She wrapped her hand around his arm as he led the way towards a red-painted concrete building with small green plants and a stone pot full of lily pads and koi fish.

"Maybe they have coffee," Daniel said.

The inside was incredibly bright. LJ looked up. The ceiling was a glass steeple with metal trusses and the sun shone right through it, beaming down onto a wooden communal table. On top of the communal table was a rectangular vase with large, leafy plants shooting out of it. Leaning up against the exposed cement walls were dark mahogany shelves. On top of the shelves were small ceramic cups, saucers and animal figurines painted in various colors. There was a round Verichron clock with a stainless steel lining attached to a wooden base and some other curio items including a spool of thread and jewelry. Inside the shelf compartments were piles of folded fabrics in different textures, patterns and colors.

At the far end of the space was a large countertop and stools where three young women were seated. When they noticed LJ and Daniel, they stood up and bowed.

"Welcome," one of them said in English. She brought two menus to the communal table.

"Have a seat," she said. Daniel smiled at the woman and said, "Thank you," in Korean. The woman smiled back. LJ looked at Daniel, without saying anything. She opened the menu.

"I'm not hungry," she said.

"Just order something small. I'm pretty hungry."

"They don't have anything small here. They only have like chili and American cheese over rice. What the hell…"

Daniel called for a server. The same woman that had seated them walked over, smiling.

"Do you serve coffee here?" he asked.

"No, we don't. We only have tea. I'm sorry."

"It's okay."

Daniel ordered two chili bowls over rice for himself and LJ with two glasses of chilled oolong tea in ice. The woman thanked him and walked away. A few minutes later, she arrived with two trays. Each had white rice with chili and cheese, and a side of miso soup full of mushrooms. LJ did not eat.

"I was out with some Korean guys last night," she said.

"Yeah? Was it fun?"

"They said that they hated seeing Korean girls dating white guys."

"Yeah, I keep hearing that, too."

"They give me a list of reasons, one of them being that there are less Korean women for them... But they never mention the real reason," said LJ.

"What's that?"

"They just think about dick sizes."

Daniel looked up from his food.

"Have you seen that movie, *Woman on the Beach* by Hong Sang-soo?" she asked.

"No."

"There's a scene with these two guys and a girl. Both guys are into her. And the guys complain about her having dated German men while she was living in Germany. And one of the guys gets really pissed and shouts that having a big dick doesn't mean anything. It was actually really refreshing to see it on screen cause when I talk to guys, they get a little protective and won't be straight with me—that's precisely their insecurity. Thing is, though, in my experience, dick sizes and race have nothing to do with each other. But this is something most men get hung up on. Pun not intended."

LJ and Daniel went into a convenience store and bought two cans of beer. They cracked it open and walked up a steep, concrete road. After finishing the beers, they abandoned the cans on a cement ledge that ran over a brick wall. The houses on the concrete hill were heavily guarded with black painted steel fences. LJ pointed at the highest point of the neighborhood. There were paper Buddha lanterns hanging from steel scaffolding on the rooftop.

"Let's go there," she said.

Daniel and LJ hiked past dozens of abandoned furniture outside of the houses. They pointed at the furniture and mentioned how that bed, nightstand, flat screen and chair were all perfectly useful and decent pieces.

"Well, it takes a lot of waste to keep up with trends," LJ said. They walked past an abandoned white building.

"I could live here probably. I'll just stay in Seoul and move in here. No one will know," Daniel said.

"The mold and asbestos would kill you."

"There's none of that here. This is an amazing building."

They finally reached the gate of the building with the Buddha lanterns. The wind was stronger at the top of the hill. There was a house with a green sliding glass door and a wooden veranda to the far left. The yard was full of various colored stones, and a patch of grass. On it was a large wooden bench cut from a single massive trunk, down vertically. LJ and Daniel walked over to the bench and looked down past the stone ledge. The city seemed covered in a sunlit mist. They sat on the bench below the paper lanterns. The wind made the paper tails of the lanterns flutter. Daniel and LJ sat still and listened. A monk wearing a green sweater and gray pants stepped out of the house and put her shoes on. She turned and bowed at LJ and Daniel. LJ and Daniel dipped their heads in her direction. The monk reached for a yellow bucket, walked across the driveway and entered a different building on the opposite end.

"Do you think we're trespassing?" Daniel asked.

"They're monks. They can't be trespassed," LJ replied.

"How do you feel right now?" Daniel asked.

"I feel alright. Do you think these lanterns were hung up here because of the sound they make in the wind?"

"Of course," Daniel said. They both sat in silence and listened to the fluttering. A couple of minutes passed.

Daniel reached down and picked out a bunch of white stones and made a small pile. LJ reached down and selected all the dark blue stones in her vicinity and made a pile next to his.

"I've been thinking about your house," Daniel said digging into his pocket. He pulled out a sheet of paper with an ink sketch of a house.

"I can't see you in a steel and glass house with modern conveniences. I can only see you inside a space that's been around for a really long time."

Daniel pointed at his drawing. It was a modestly-sized house with a façade of two windows and a door.

"It's held together by timber and large mill cut columns, and paned glass windows that are like, a hundred years old but sturdy enough to push open, and when they do, they open up in large sections. Outside, you can hear only natural sounds like trees, water and birds. And the floors will have some squeaks here and there when you walk over them because they're meant to creak that way. It's to signify time. And maybe a large desk for you. And a typewriter so you can write on it."

"Wow. This is lovely. What kind of tree is this?" LJ asked, pointing to a tree beside the house.

"I don't know. A pear blossom maybe."

Daniel folded it and handed it to LJ.

"Thanks, Daniel."

"Alright, let's go," he said. "We'll share a cab back.

"Okay."

The inside of the cab was quiet. LJ could hear Daniel breathing. Fifteen minutes later, the cab pulled up at Daniel's apartment.

"You coming?" he asked.

"Um. Okay."

"What time's your flight tomorrow?"

"In the afternoon, around two."

LJ followed Daniel up two flights and entered. Inside were white walls, a large glass table in the center of the studio with rolls of sketches, small wooden models, paintings and loose sheets of paper all over the floor.

"Don't slip," Daniel said.

"You have anything to drink?" LJ asked.

"Yeah. I have some wine."

"I'm gonna borrow some of your clothes."

LJ went over to Daniel's dresser and pulled out a pair of shorts. She went to his closet and pulled a light blue button down shirt. Daniel grabbed the wine from the fridge and cracked it open. He brought two glasses over to the bed and sat beside her. He reached for a black shoebox on his desk and placed it on LJ's lap.

LJ opened the box while Daniel poured wine into each glass. Inside the box were prints of photographs taken in Hapcheon. There was one of the white puppy, another of LJ's hand touching greens inside a plastic basin. There was one of LJ's grandmother and her grandfather sitting together on the veranda.

"It was good that we went on a trip while I was still here," LJ said. "These prints are beautiful."

"Yeah."

"What are you going to do with them?" LJ asked.

"I don't know. What's there to do with pictures, really?"

Daniel touched LJ's shoulder.

"I'm tired," she said. LJ stretched out on the bed and turned away from him.

"Are you going to sleep?"

"Yes."

LJ listened to Daniel get up and walk to the other side of the room. He switched off the light then returned to bed. LJ felt Daniel's hand move across her stomach as his arm wrapped around her waist. He pulled her towards him then put his mouth on her bare shoulder. LJ gasped. He turned her body to have her face him and pressed his mouth against hers. LJ pulled away.

"What are you doing?" LJ asked.

"What do you mean?" Daniel asked.

He lifted LJ's shirt and dug his head underneath it.

"What about Mona?" she asked.

"What about her?" he said, head still inside moving towards her breast.

LJ shoved Daniel's head out of the shirt. Daniel sat up, kneeling on the bed, looking at LJ. LJ looked back without saying anything. Daniel put his hands on LJ's hips and pulled the shorts down. He pushed her legs apart and dug his face in between.

The light from the street lamp came in through the window past the white drapes. It was orange like all the lights LJ had seen in Seoul. LJ grew sad at the sight. She put her hand over her eyes to keep the tears from flowing. They made their way down the sides of her head and stained the pillow.

"I don't want to leave tomorrow."

Daniel entered LJ and dug his face into her neck. LJ sniffled.

"Stop crying. It's not fun when you cry."

Several minutes passed. LJ looked at Daniel's face in the dark as he moved inside her. He pushed her knee over to the left and pushed down on both of her legs with his hand and the weight of his torso as he changed positions. LJ winced.

"Is that uncomfortable?" he asked.

"No, it's fine."

"Okay."

Daniel changed the angle slightly then penetrated again. As LJ came loudly, Daniel clamped her mouth shut with his hand.

"Shut up. My neighbors are going to hear you."

LJ shook herself free and slapped Daniel's face several times with both hands. He grabbed both her hands then sped up. LJ yelled again. Daniel pulled out and came on her stomach.

They lay quietly for a few minutes without speaking.

"Hey, what do you want to do when you go back to New York?" Daniel finally asked.

"I don't know. What do you want to do when you come to New York?" she asked.

Daniel turned and looked at her.

"Your program here is nearly up. You can join me in the fall," she said.

"I want to. But I don't know what I would do there."

"There's always something," LJ said turning away.

"Yeah, but I don't want to do just anything. Like, I don't want to work at some fucking café or something. I want to work in a real office and have real designers as colleagues."

Daniel didn't speak for a minute. He got up and went to the sink. He grabbed a sheet of paper towel, brought it over to LJ and wiped the semen from her stomach.

"What do you want to do there?" Daniel asked.

"I want to publish my manuscript. And write. I'm going to write essays and get published."

"You want to be a struggling writer?" he asked.

"I *am* a struggling writer. But I don't want to struggle when I get back home. I don't plan on struggling. I just want to read books and write," LJ said.

"Well. Sounds like you have a plan then," Daniel said. He turned onto his back and faced the ceiling.

Daniel shut his eyes then turned his back towards LJ.

"I'd like to be there. But not sure how or when," he said.

LJ turned her back to Daniel. The curves of their backs touched. She reached for sounds from outside and inside. She could only make out Daniel's breath. It slowly grew steady and eventually became a gentle snore. LJ lay awake and listened until she grew heavy with sleep.

90

Religion and Sisters

Oskar enters the deli with his thermos. He makes eye contact with me then points at the hot water dispenser. I nod my head. He fills his thermos then walks over to me.

"Your family is Korean, yes?"

"Yes, sir."

"Do they own this store?"

"No, they do not."

"What do your parents do, LJ?"

"They work. They work in the furniture business, so they are always going out of business."

"It's a difficult business," Oskar says. He reaches into his pocket and takes out a Lipton tea bag. He tears it open and drops the bag into the thermos.

"Did your parents push you hard to study?" Oskar asks.

"No. Not really. Sometimes, but not really with studying. They're very religious Protestants though, so, I don't really talk to them if I can help it."

"You are not a Protestant?"

"No. I'm not anything. Are you a Protestant?" I ask.

"I am Catholic," Oskar says.

"That's okay, too. We all need something, I guess."

"Are you a Buddhist?"

"No. I don't practice Buddhism. I like Buddhism, though," I say.

I walk out onto the floor and pickup a napkin and a white wrapper. I bring them behind the register and throw them into the trash bin.

Three Filipinas emerge loudly from behind him. I recognize two of them from the other day. They walk over to the register with bananas and sandwiches wrapped in wax paper. Oskar tips his hat at me then leaves.

"How are you?" I ask.

"You remember our faces, ah?" one of them says. "That is because you are Asian. We are sisters."

The woman hands me a fifty-dollar bill. I return her change. The ladies place the food items on an orange tray and carry it towards the seating area chatting. Everything they say is loud with emphasis. The sound of their chatter cheers me up.

A young white girl with gray dreadlocks, an eggplant tattoo on her arm and a nose ring asks for American Spirits.

"The yellow ones," she says.

"I.D.?"

The girl opens up an orange pouch with a zipper. She hands me her Minnesota driver's license.

"Okay."

She hands me a twenty and I hand her, her change. She turns and walks away. I see a quote knitted onto her backpack: "Apparently anything is possible today." –Mark Twain

A white man in a blue windbreaker, gold-rimmed glasses and a baseball cap walks in yelling things. It is hard to understand what it is that he wants so I listen to him carefully, waiting to catch the right words and figure it out.

"Are you impolite? No. You must always be polite. Thank you. Haha! Yeah. Thursdays. Haha! Polite. Be polite. I want a twenty. Girls? Yeck!"

The man hands me two ten-dollar bills. I open the register and hand him a twenty-dollar bill. The man turns around and leaves, still yelling many things at once. Mr. Kim walks in and waves at me then salutes Mr. Moy. Mr. Moy nods his head then goes to the wall phone and dials.

"Mr. Choi? Yes, so-so today. Thirteen hundred. Okay. Thank you. Bye." Mr. Moy hangs up.

"Okay, LJ. I'll see you next Sunday."

"Bye Mr. Moy."

Mr. Moy steps down from the register platform then heads out the door, headed for Penn Station.

I look down at my phone and see an email from Chuck.

He says he's in town from L.A. editing his film with his co-director and editor.

"Come join us for dinner. My musician friend is coming to meet you so wear eye makeup. Here is the address."

I walk to the back of the store, grab a bottle of Smart Water and raise it in the air for Mr. Kim to see. Mr. Kim waves his hand at me. I put the water in my bag. I punch "1.00" into the register opposite his and drop a dollar in.

Out on Seventh Avenue, Oskar is leaning out of the ice cream truck in his white cap, photographing something. I look at the direction of where he is shooting and see a trash bin and people walking. I walk up to the truck and call his name. He says nothing.

"Oskar!" I shout.

"Oh, hello, LJ."

"What are you photographing?"

"I am photographing the corner."

"Why?"

"It is my hobby."

I laugh.

"Okay."

"Do you want a sample?" he asks me.

"No. I'm good."

"Come now. Just a little bit. What do you want? Vanilla? Chocolate? Or combination?"

"No. I'm stuffed. Big Phil brought a pizza for me not too long ago. I gotta head over to Brooklyn for dinner now. I'll see you next weekend."

"Okay, my friend. Take care."

I walk up Thirty-fourth Street and into an Old Navy. I grab a gray knitted sweater and walk towards the fitting rooms. A girl unlocks a room and lets me in. Inside, I throw the sweater onto the bench, take out a black skirt and a dark turquoise top. I get changed. I pull out my compact and reapply makeup. I untie my hair and let it down. I shove my jeans and red t-shirt into my tote bag. I walk out of the fitting room and put the sweater back on the rack and leave the store.

On my way to the F train, through the bustling crowd, I feel a hand grab my left elbow. I turn.

A small man with blue eyes and red sunburnt skin peeling peers into my face, squeezing my arm. He's wearing a dark green overcoat and a navy blue wool cap, giving off a strong stench.

"Excuse me miss, excuse me miss, can I lick your pussy?"

I yank my arm away.

"Get the fuck away from me," I say.

The man looks back at me in horror as I turn to walk.

"Go back to China, you fucking bitch!" he yells.

A few men and woman turn and look at me as I race towards the F train down the steps at Herald Square Station, eyes burning hot with angry tears.

91

Friends

At Prospect Park, I follow the address in Chuck's text message and arrive at a duplex brownstone. I ring the doorbell. A woman greets me at the door with a baby in her arms.

"Hello. I'm Dana," she says.

"Hi Dana. I'm LJ."

"Come on in. The boys are in the editing room."

Dana offers me red wine.

"Are you hungry?" Dana asks. She has a soothing accent. I can't identify where it's from.

"I'm okay for now."

Tim enters the room and asks Dana to help him change the baby's sweater. Dana excuses herself. Chuck enters and gives me a hug.

"Did you get lost?" Chuck asks.

"A little. I was daydreaming on the subway."

"What were you daydreaming about?" he asked.

"I don't know. Nothing, really."

Chuck laughs.

"I'm gonna write a poem entitled 'Daydreaming on the Subway about Nothing Really.'"

A tall white guy wearing a blue and black, checkered T-shirt enters.

"LJ, this is Domenico. He's our editor. Domenico, LJ."

Domenico waves at me then pours more red wine into his glass. He invites me to come join the guys in the editing room.

"No, I don't want to impose."

"No, please come. Sit down. Here is a chair."

Domenico pulls out a chair and puts a bowl of cherries in front of me.

"Thank you."

The editing room's walls are painted in a light sea green. Domenico plays different soundtracks against driving sequences. I make a point that I hadn't seen too many moving scenes where the shot was taken from the back seat, pulling away from the starting point.

"Yeah," Tim says. Somebody calls the computer on Skype. Domenico pushes answer. A face appears on the other end.

"Hi, Bill."

"Hey, guys. What's new?"

I excuse myself and leave the room. Out in the living room, I see Dana sitting on a stool with Sylvie in her arms.

"Hey."

"Hi. How is it in there?"

"Things are happening, I guess. I got bored." I chuckle.

"Yeah. And I'm getting hungry."

The baby smiles at me. I smile back. She smiles even wider.

"What's the baby's name?" I ask.

"Sylvie."

"That's a sweet name."

Dana smiles at Sylvie and bounces her gently on her lap.

"Let me show you where I work," Dana says. She stands up and walks towards a door that leads into another room.

Inside, the first thing I see is a large fish tank.

"Those are our fish," she says.

"Are they guppies?"

"No. They're zebra fish, I think they are called."

"Oh, cool."

"We originally bought the tank to raise newts but they didn't make it, poor things."

"Oh, that's too bad."

"Yeah."

I look around at the objects on the table beside the fish tank. There are feathers, rocks, and seashells.

"Are you an anthropologist?" I ask.

"Ha ha. No, but I studied it in college. Wow. How'd you know?" Dana laughs.

"I don't know. Just a feeling."

"I'm an improv instructor now. I teach at Queens College. I do that and I DJ on occasion. I'm also a musician."

"All of that still seem like anthropology," I tell her.

"Yeah. I guess they are."

We walk back out into the living space. Dana sits on the piano stool again. I lean against the couch and look through some of the books that are inside a brown box. They are all Paul Auster novels.

"A Paul Auster fan?" I ask.

"Yeah, I haven't read any of his works yet. A friend of ours just left that here a couple days ago. She moved to London."

"I see."

"So, what do you do, LJ?"

"On the weekdays I sit at a desk. On the weekends I stand by a register."

Dana smiles.

"Okay. What else?"

"Oh. I write. I'm a writer, I guess," I say.

"I see. So now I see how you know Chuck," she says, bouncing Sylvie gently on her lap.

"Yes. We met in Seoul. We were in the same writing circle."

"Oh, awesome. What were you doing in Seoul? Studying?"

"No. I was translating Korean literature."

"Oh wow."

"Yeah. It was pretty depressing."

"A lot of the literature from my country are painful to read, too."

"Where are you from?"

"I was born in Uruguay."

I look down at Sylvie. The baby smiles at me again.

"She's very sweet, your little girl," I say to Dana.

"She's just three months now. Do you have any children?"

"No. No children. I'm twenty-three years old. I can't have children."

"Yeah. Take your time. There's plenty of time."

I look at a book resting on the piano stand. "HUNDERTWASSER" is written across it in big red letters. The drawing on the cover is beautiful. It's bright, and full of energy.

"Are you working on any projects now?" Dana asks.

"I'm just trying to get my manuscript published. But it's hard out there."

"That's wonderful. Congratulations."

"Thank you."

"Did someone sponsor you?"

"There was a grant that I applied for. It gives money to

translators and it's supposed to promote international awareness or whatever. I got that a year ago and worked in Seoul. I've only been back a little over a month."

"That sounds great."

"Yeah, but, it means nothing in the end. I'm still struggling day to day."

"Things will work out."

"Thanks."

"Okay. This is getting ridiculous. Let's get the guys out of there and go to dinner," Dana says.

We go to an Italian place. During our walk over to the restaurant, I mention a scene that Chuck had shown me back in Seoul.

"The scene at the bar where the guy is just improvising this song out of nowhere. It was amazing. I can't shake that image. It was so intense. Who was that guy? The one with the eyes," I say to Tim.

"Yo, Chuck, LJ likes the scene with Lonnie improvising that song," Tim says, turning back at Chuck and Domenico.

"Oh yeah? Yeah, that scene's intense. We're gonna keep it, I think," Chuck says.

"Yeah. Let's keep it," Tim says. A cool breeze hits our backs as we walk.

"Look at the trees, LJ," Dana says. I look up. A tunnel of green leaves envelops us. Dana says that she'd initially wanted to move to Brooklyn Heights but that she loved trees so much that she had to settle for this area.

At the restaurant, we order two bottles of red wine—one from Sicily and the other from California. I get drunk. The guys chat about films. Chuck mentions one film that left an impression on him:

"It was about two kids having a baby. And there's this scene where the girl is playing with a doll while she's in labor. That movie was, oh my god. So intense," he says.

"That sounds fucked up," I say.

"What is this," Tim asks, grabbing one of the bottles.

"That's the California," Dana says.

"What am I drinking now?" Tim asks.

"I don't remember," she says.

"Whatever." Tim pours it into his glass.

I excuse myself and step out for a smoke. I inhale then exhale, thinking about the pain my head is in. My body aches. The day-to-day worries over the debt from student loans, not being properly employed, not having health insurance, and getting offers for shitty jobs with shitty pay accumulate. I feel my nose sting as my eyes well up.

I turn around and peer inside the glass window into the restaurant. I see waiters stacking chairs behind my friends. Dana and Tim are speaking with their faces close to each other's, with the baby nestled in between them. Domenico is gesticulating loudly with his hands, telling Chuck a story. I stand below the restaurant awning and take a drag from my cigarette. The street light in front of me goes from green to yellow to red.

92

Flight

LJ woke up to the strong morning's light. It invaded the room and touched almost everything, including her face. She looked over to her left and saw Daniel still sleeping.

LJ quietly gathered her clothes, went into the bathroom, tied her hair and washed her face. When she returned to his room, Daniel was in the kitchen drinking water.

"I should head back. I have a plane to catch," she said.

"Sure."

Daniel walked LJ to the door and kissed her on the top of her head.

"I'll see you then," she said before closing the door.

Outside the building, LJ hailed a cab then headed back to her apartment where her suitcases were already packed and waiting. She hopped the airport bus from the stop near her apartment. Forty-five minutes later, it arrived at Incheon International Airport where she checked in on a one-way flight back to JFK Airport.

93

Time

I return to the table.

"You promised me a sexy musician," I say to Chuck. "I wore eye makeup." I blink my eyes rapidly in his face.

"Shit, yeah. He's a flake," Chuck says. "Sorry."

"Yeah, man. Where's your friend?" Domenico asks.

"The guy said he couldn't make it. Some gig downtown. So I was just like, dude, you're a douche."

"It's okay," I say. "I don't really care."

"Just go with Domenico," Chuck says.

"I'm gay," Domenico says. "But yeah, I'll go with you."

Dana gets up to go to the bathroom.

"Hey, after I leave for Cali, keep seeing these guys," Chuck says. "Talk to Dana. She's been all over the world. She used to wear gold paint and stand like a statue in the middle of squares in Rome and Paris for money. She used to sing at these crazy underground bars all over Eastern Europe. She's a cool chick."

"Yeah, I mean, she seems amazing. She's got such an earthy quality to her," I say.

"I know. You can feel it."

Dana returns from the bathroom.

"You just settled the check didn't you," Chuck says to her.

"Yeah. Don't worry about it. Let's go," she says.

On our way back, the guys chat about Michel Gondry and Gus van Sant. Dana and I quietly walk beside them.

"Do you work tomorrow?" Dana asks me.

"Yes."

"Where do you work?"

"At a PR firm in Midtown. I do some copy editing there."

"I see."

"I mean, it's pretty mind-numbing. Really awful stuff, but it's a job. I was at an interview on Friday but I don't want to work at a law firm. And this weekend job that I have is pretty taxing but the deli is pretty fun and interesting. I can't do it forever, though."

"Give it time," Dana says.

"Yeah. I just feel like, with anything I want to do right now, there's a huge roadblock. And the things I don't want to do are the very things that'll feed me in the long run. But I wonder if I even want to be alive doing the kinds of things that are so-called options today."

"That's alright. Just get into everything. Try on all the hats."

"Yeah, I mean. I'm just still so new at all this," I say. Dana nods her head. I feel like a huge hole appeared in my chest and air is tunneling through it.

"Everyone around me tries so hard at turning me into *something*, but I don't want to be anything specifically. Which is why I'm resisting everything right now. I think that's better. Better to resist being turned into something and losing the significance of a real person, don't you think?"

Back at the apartment, Dana and Tim pick mint leaves from their garden out front. They give each of us some. I put the mint leaves inside my jacket pocket then step inside, following

Dana's lead. The guys reenter the editing room again and invite me to join. Inside, they turn on *JFK* and skip around to different scenes and have an avid discussion about each. I leave the room again and sit on the couch. I see Dana sitting by the piano, looking at some music. I lean my head back against the couch and close my eyes. I can feel myself clinging to something, like I don't want to fall.

Suddenly I am not clinging. I'm surrounded by a padded darkness and remain there immobile, wordless—as nothing.

From a distance through the dark cloud, I can hear Chuck talking to Dana—something about hailing a cab, something about not knowing where I live.

"I'm just a bit worried about her," he says.

"She seems like a tough girl," Dana replies.

I sleep.

Acknowledgements

. Thank you to the following whose support made this book possible (in alphabetical order): Bruce and Ju-chan Fulton, Loren Goodman, Mark Hussey, John Jung, Fulbright Korea, Catherine Min, and Charles North.

About the Author

Grace Jung is a New York-based writer, translator and film producer. She is the author of *The Moon Hangs Like a Stupid Mistake* and *Gethsemane*. Her fiction has been published in The Cortland Review and Molotov Cocktail. Her translation of Yi Sang's poetry is published in *Acta Koreana*. She also translated Lee Cheong-jun's book *Worm Story* (basis for Lee Chang-dong's *Secret Sunshine*) which is forthcoming at Merwin Asia Publishing. She is a recipient of the Academy of American Poets Prize, and is a former Fulbright scholar. She is currently producing a feature documentary film entitled A-Town Boyz and writing her second novel.

www.ingramcontent.com/pod-product-compliance
Lightning Source LLC
Chambersburg PA
CBHW021524250626
47154CB00006BA/1960